MISFITS

The eight short stories in this collection are all about people who feel isolated, cut off, even looked down on, because they're different. They find life tough, because they don't conform – in their backgrounds, their personalities, their names or their companions. They are misfits.

Also available from Methuen Teens

The Changeover by Margaret Mahy
I'm Not Your Other Half by Caroline B. Cooney
Nick's October by Alison Prince
The Teenagers' Handbook by Peter Murphy and Kitty Grime
Haunted by Judith St George
Fire and Hemlock by Diana Wynne Jones
Masque for a Queen by Moira Miller
Badger by Anthony Masters
Rainbows of the Gutter by Rukshana Smith
Flight in Yiktor by André Norton
Taking Terri Mueller by Norma Fox Mazer
Firebrats: The Burning Land by Barbara and Scott Siegel
Firebrats: Survivors by Barbara and Scott Siegel

Misfits

••••

AN ANTHOLOGY OF
SHORT STORIES
EDITED BY
PEGGY WOODFORD

••••

Methuen

Acknowledgement: The title of Frances Thomas's story is taken from Walter J. Turner's poem 'Romance' and four verses are quoted in the story by kind permission of Messrs Sidgwick & Jackson.

First published in 1984
by The Bodley Head Ltd
This Methuen Teens paperback edition first published 1988
by Methuen Children's Books Ltd
11 New Fetter Lane, London EC4P 4EE
This collection and *Misfits* copyright © 1984 Peggy Woodford
King copyright © 1984 Jon Blake
Threads copyright © 1984 Jane Gardam
Outside copyright © 1984 R. M. Lamming
The French Exchange copyright © 1984 Penelope Lively
Mackerel copyright © 1984 Emma Smith
Chimborazo, Cotopaxi . . . copyright © 1984 Frances Thomas
Jack, Vince, Jo-Ann and the Raving Revvers copyright © 1984 John Wain
Printed in Great Britain
by Cox & Wyman Ltd, Reading

ISBN 0 416 09672 7

CONTENTS

Misfits, 1
PEGGY WOODFORD

The French Exchange, 28
PENELOPE LIVELY

King, 45
JON BLAKE

Threads, 62
JANE GARDAM

Mackerel, 72
EMMA SMITH

Jack, Vince, Jo-Ann, and the Raving Revvers, 96
JOHN WAIN

Outside, 130
R. M. LAMMING

Chimborazo, Cotopaxi . . ., 147
FRANCES THOMAS

About the Authors, 169

Misfits
PEGGY WOODFORD

••••

My grandmother, who smokes cigars and runs a home for battered birds in her bungalow, once gave us a game called Misfits. (She couldn't have chosen better, given the nature of our family.) This game really taxes the brain.

Three or more of you get dealt seven cards each, and on the cards there are separate parts of a whole collection of characters: the hats, heads, bodies, legs of a Scotsman, a monkey, a policeman, a pirate, a dancing girl etc. Playing in turn, and taking new cards, you build up a crazy being consisting, say, of a top hat, a baby's face, a monkey's body, and the legs of an astronaut. The person who matches the second leg gets the trick. I told you it taxed the brain.

Our cards are dog-eared, we played it so much as little kids. My seven-year-old brother Rory still gets a kick out of it, crying 'Yuk' in delight as the Misfits are misfitted. I now find the whole game too near the bone. I mean, take a look at our family.

Point one. We're called Slaughters. Now I know there exist plenty of people who've survived the name Slaughter and even become famous. The other day I noticed there was a journalist called Slaughter; I keep telling myself she's called Slaughter and she's done O.K. But she hasn't got an 's' on the end, so people don't think of her as a violent verb.

Point two. My mother started going to an adult education centre half way through her family and this gave her new ideas. My elder brothers are called John and Robert. By the time my sister and I came along we were called Selina and Seth. *Seth*. It's a ridiculous name. Seth Slaughters. I don't know how I've survived fourteen years.

Point three. My father started his own firm a couple of years ago. Before that he was a civil servant of a sort. He worked in the Sewage Department. Then he decided to branch out on his own, and went into activated sludge. Slaughters' Sludge.

It's too much.

I liked Miss Wellington. She always said what she thought. When she took us on class outings, she didn't nag us for fooling about. She'd give us a meeting time, very firmly, and then tell us those who wanted to stick with her were welcome to. As a result, most people stuck with her. And surprise, surprise, it was actually interesting.

Towards the end of my time in her class, she took us to the local art gallery. There we were at one point, standing just the two of us in front of a painting of an old bloke with warts, when she said suddenly:

'So what do you think you'll do for a career, Seth?'

'I want to be a doctor.'

There was a snort from her. She was laughing.

'I'd advise you to change your name, in that case. You might not inspire confidence otherwise.'

I must be dumb. I really must be dumb. You won't

believe this, but I had never thought of it that way. Doctor Slaughters Mrs Bloggs . . . etc. Big joke.

Miss Wellington stopped laughing. 'Listen, Seth. Don't let your name bug you. If it does, change it. There are quite enough problems in life without adding to them with something as maddening as an unfortunate name. Wait till you leave school perhaps, then change it. Your life'll be changing anyway then, you might as well cash in. Anyway, let's go and look at the Gainsborough.'

Miss Wellington left the school at the end of that term. When I gave her the present my mother had insisted on sending me with—a boring old box of chocolates and she'd had seven already—Miss Wellington said: 'Names are important. Choose a good one.' She smiled. 'I'm getting married this summer, but I'm keeping my own name. Wellington's more interesting than Smith, don't you agree? And thanks for giving me these. I mean it.' Her eyes were sort of greeny-yellow. I suddenly realized that she wasn't old at all. 'I've enjoyed my first proper job,' she said.

S.P.A.N. The Society for People with Awful Names. I wrote SPAN several times in different ways in my rough book. It looked good. I didn't hear a word of that French lesson, and hurried home after school to find Selina. She was unenthusiastic.

'What's in a name? No one cares enough to join a society.'

'How do you know?'

'Well, I wouldn't bother. I don't mind being Slaughters. Anyway, I'll get married and leave it behind.'

I gazed at her. She makes me sick. Just because she's nearly seventeen and in love with the head boy at my school, she talks like that. I can't understand what Sam Willis sees in her. All his dates with her must be blind.

'Selina Slaughters Sam Willis.'

She stared back at me. 'Oh, clever clogs. So original.'

'These days intelligent women keep their own surnames when they get married.'

'Quite the little feminist sympathizer, I see. Well, I'm not interested. I'll be delighted when I lose the name Slaughters.'

'You just said you didn't care.'

'All right, so I do mind a bit.'

'In that case, why not be more interested in my SPAN idea?'

'Oh, grow up, Seth.'

There's absolutely no point carrying on a conversation with Selina these days. I don't know if it's because of love or an inadequate diet—she's become a vegetarian—but she's ratty most of the time.

Soon after this, I began a list of people with awful names. I started off with names like ours connected with death and found in our telephone directory:

Slay (3)
Slaymaker (5)
Death (8) (plus lots of PANs who'd changed it to De'ath, thus fooling nobody)
Deadman (33!)
Kill (10)
Killman (2)
Killingback (16)

I noticed near the Ks that there were four lots called Kick and five called Kicks. Pretty stupid names to endure school life with—I could just hear the chorus: *John Kicks so let's kick him.* I went on looking for names that meant trouble at school. Smelly. Smellie. Seven lots of Smellies in fact; unbelievable. Bog, Bogg, Boggs. (I ruled out Chinese names; they seem quite happy about being called Loo and Pong.) Gay. That was a sad name to have, because not so long ago it would have been fine. Cock— dozens of them. Cocks—even more; Cocking, Cockshut, Cockwell. Bottom, Bottome. Peed.

There were so many awful names, I couldn't believe it. I began to spend hours with directories, trying to find new ones. But all the time I was thinking, how could people endure lifetimes of being called, say, Alfred Cock. A. Cock, Esq. Cock major, Cock minor. I mean, you'd never even survive your schooldays. I began to wonder why people with grade one awful names (Slaughters was definitely grade two) hadn't changed them to something bearable.

But it would be typical of the average person's approach to life if it hadn't occurred to them. Or they could be the grin-and-bear-it brigade. There they were, growing skins several inches thick and/or becoming total neurotics, when they could turn from Alfred Cock to Alfred Cary, or Carlisle. Or any damn name they liked which didn't make introductions a torture.

'And what's your name, dear?'

'Gladys Smellie.' Or whatever. What a life.

Another thing. It's funny how often people with awful surnames seem to choose revolting Christian names for their kids. Perhaps it's the in-for-a-penny, in-for-a-pound attitude. More likely, their taste in names is perverted by being a Smellie from the cradle onwards. And being Smellie for generations can't do much for the soul either.

Someone had given me, one Christmas, a red plastic

card index box plus cards and alphabetical dividers. So I put the names and addresses of all the PANs I found on cards, and felt very efficient. It took me a whole evening. I decided to keep the contents of my box secret from my family. This is difficult in our house, because all of us are dead curious; opening drawers and fiddling about is our besetting sin. We draw the line at opening each other's post, though; anything sealed up is left alone. I sealed up my card index with Sellotape just to make sure, and hid it on top of my wardrobe.

Then nothing happened for a bit. It wasn't that I lost interest, I just lost push. It was when a boy called Alexander Pigg joined my class—(A. Pigg again—don't parents *ever* consider what initials do to a name?)—that the whole SPAN thing got off the ground.

Alex Pigg had been moved to our school because of victimization, he told me one lunch break.

'Victimization? Over your name?'

'That started it. I was all right until I got to the Main School, because they used Christian names until then. From this year onwards we had to use surnames. The bullies got going.' Alex had a dropping voice which made him sound a bit wet when he wasn't really.

'Why didn't you change your name when you changed school?'

'No one thought of it.' He frowned. 'I'm too young to do that, aren't I?'

I looked at him. I didn't know the answer, but in that moment I decided I'd find out as soon as possible. 'I'm going to change mine the moment I can.'

Alex had blue eyes, quite small; his red hair and pink skin were unfortunately the right colour for a pig.

6

'Listen, Alex. If you changed your name to something quite different, like—like MacTavish—no one would ever tease you again.' I don't know why I chose Mac-Tavish, but it pleased him.

'Alexander MacTavish.' He looked at me and grinned.

I couldn't ask my parents about how you changed your name by deed poll. They were proud of the name Slaughters or at least they pretended to be. Besides, they were best avoided at the moment. The activated sludge market was sluggish; Dad was very gloomy about it and Mum gave her energies to cheering him up which left her kids out in the cold. I thought of asking Selina's advice but decided against it. Though she's gone back on to meat again, her temper hasn't improved much. I asked her how things were with Sam Willis and was given the works. I left her to it before she'd finished ranting on.

Mum always telephones the Town Hall when she wants to know things, so I gave it a try.

'Well, I couldn't say, dear,' said the receptionist. 'There's no department on my list for that sort of thing. By deed poll. What's that?'

'I don't know exactly. That's why I'm asking.'

'Well, dear, try the police. Or the Post Office. They might know.' She had the sort of voice that made you feel she was patting her hair or doing her nails or something while she talked. 'Best of luck, anyway. I always wanted to change my name when I was a kid. Luckily Mr Right came along and did it for me.'

'What was your name, then?'

'Aha. That would be telling.' She gave a silly laugh and rang off. Some women make you sick.

I suppose I was getting obsessed with this name business. I wanted to start my Society for People with Awful Names, but I couldn't quite work out the format. One thing I *had* to know was the correct procedure for changing your name. If nothing else, SPAN could pass that information around.

The local police station was great. 'Why are you so interested in changing your name then, sonny? Done something you want us to forget?' Ha, ha. I rang off.

Finally Alex (he was dead keen on the idea of SPAN now) and I went to a small post office near our school. There was a grey-haired man behind the glass barricade, with a kind face. He was checking figures when we went in, having seen that the post office was empty. We waited until he jotted down a figure and looked up.

'It would be quicker if I used a calculator but I like exercising the old brain.' He smiled. 'What can I do for you?'

'We wanted to find out about changing your name by deed poll. Nobody seems to know.' I waited for him to make a crack, but he just listened. I blurted out: 'We've got awful surnames and we want to change them.'

'Don't blame you. Funnily enough, you've come to the right man. I know all about it because my nephew's just changed his name. He's a pop singer—well, he tries to be one—and he changed his not long ago from David Harris to Rocco Rocker.' He stopped.

'Rocco Rocker. Sounds good, Rocco Rocker,' I said, to keep the conversation going. Success at last. Someone knew!

'Rocco's an Italian name.' An old lady had come in and he turned to serve her. He stamped her pension book and gave her a wad of notes, chatting to her about her dog as he did so. When she'd gone, he offered us a Polo mint.

'Yes. Changing your name. Well, you'll have to wait until you're eighteen. Then, you announce you don't want to be known as Joe Smith any more; your name's Cary Grant. Or whatever. Dead easy.'

We gazed at him, disappointed. He couldn't be right.

'Come to think of it, Cary Grant's real name wasn't Cary Grant. It was Archie Leach. So, boys, wait until you're eighteen, and you can do the same. Then you inform everyone—the relevant authorities, the bank, British Telecom, your friends—all your contacts. Rocco had a good idea. You know those cards saying Mr and Mrs So-and-so have moved; well, Rocco just sent out cards saying David Harris would in future be known as Rocco Rocker. Says he might change it again, later on.'

'But is that legal?' I didn't fully believe the man.

'It's legal. I promise you, it's legal.'

'What about this deed poll business? Did Rocco have one of those?'

'You don't have to by law, but you can if you want. It's just a piece of paper, stating the change, and witnessed by another person. I was Rocco's witness.'

'But—' I had visualized a deed poll looking like those certificates you get for passing music exams. Stiff cream paper, posh writing. 'You mean, any piece of paper? Or do you have to get a special form from the government?'

'Look, my lad, you're a great one for making difficulties when there aren't any.' He put his mints back in his pocket. 'Any piece of paper will do.'

'Oh. So it really is dead easy.'

'Once you're eighteen.'

'Three and a half years.'

There was a pause while he tidied up some forms. We were just leaving when he said:

'So what are your names then?'

'Seth Slaughters.'

'Alex Pigg.'

He stared at us. 'That's rich, boys. Seth Slaughters Alex Pigg. That's rich, that is.' He shook his head, starting to laugh. 'I'm not surprised you want to change your names. Seth Slaughters Pigg . . . ' He was still enjoying the joke when we got out of the door.

Now I had a reason to found SPAN. I could tell all those poor people called Cockshut and Muck and all the rest that changing your name was a pushover. Even if that's all SPAN could achieve, it was something. After all, look at Alex. He'd felt a lot better now he had hope. He even had a great idea. He tried to get his parents to change their name at once, then he wouldn't have to wait. They said they'd consider it, but it turned out that after all his dad didn't want to. Pigg was an old name, he said. He didn't want to see it die.

'He must be mad.'

Alex had potato and cream cheese on the end of his nose. We were eating large jacket potatoes with fillings—I had ham and sweet corn—which you can get from a take-away near the school. They're dead good. Better than anything in the school cafeteria for the same money. Alex always has the cream cheese and chives filling. He's not adventurous over food. It took me a while to persuade him to try the jacket potatoes in the first place.

'He really must be mad. He's forgotten what it was like to live through your schooldays as a Pigg.' Alex snuffled and honked as he rootled in his potato, getting a straight look from a woman on the next park bench. 'Oink, oink.'

Setting up SPAN took us a lot of effort. We had to get through to the kids, because we had the feeling grown-up PANs might behave the way the Piggs had, or tell us to get stuffed. They liked being called Smellie or Death. Good Old English Names must be Preserved. But we were sure if our letter reached any teenage Smellies or Deaths, we'd be in business.

Eventually we bashed out the following letter, after a lot of sweat and argument.

To the members of the family with the name ...., but particularly to anyone under 18. We, the undersigned (that would reassure them), have decided to found the Society for People with Awful Names, known as SPAN. These are our aims.
1. To support each other against victimization while at school etc. (Alex's suggestion)
2. To help our members by giving them the correct information on how to change their names. (My suggestion)
3. To meet together if members want to. (Alex. I was dubious.)

Please fill in the enclosed form if you're interested in joining SPAN. Membership is 50p; if you'd like a SPAN badge, send £1.00 altogether.
Hoping to hear from you.
                    Seth Slaughters (14½)
                    Alex Pigg (14)

Selina tidied up the letter for us, and helped draw up

11

the form, which had boxes for putting ticks in if you wanted info about changing your name etc. In fact, we'd never have done the letter and the form if it hadn't been for Selina turning friendly. She'd suddenly asked me, while I was mending a puncture for her: 'What happened to that idea you had for a club for people with lousy names?'

'Me and Alex have been working on it.'

'I and Alex. It's not a bad idea.'

'Thought you were against it.'

'I never said that.' She peered with me into the bowl of water, trying to find the telltale small stream of bubbles.

'I've collected loads of names from directories. We thought we'd send them all a letter. Trouble is, we've got to get it typed and photocopied.'

'I could type it for you at school. I need plenty of practice anyway. There's a photocopier at school as well; it's in the office but Miss Roper might let me use it if she felt kind.'

Bubbles rushed out of a slit. 'You must have gone over a piece of glass. Look at that.'

'No wonder it went down so fast. Who's going to pay the postage of all these letters?'

'Me and Alex have raised the money.'

'How?'

'I'm not saying.'

'Did you pinch it?'

'You can mend your own stupid puncture.'

'Oh calm down, Seth, come back.'

'You know I don't go in for stealing.'

'O.K., O.K. I wasn't serious.'

I dried the inner tube for her, sanded it, and fixed a

patch on it in silence. Then she said as I was blowing it up: 'Well, go on, how did you get your funds?'

'Don't tell anyone.'

'Why should I?'

'We made proper-looking collecting tins with SPAN on them, and wore badges made with that kit Mum gave me once, and we stood outside the station, rattling our tins.'

'You are joking.'

'I'm not.'

'Don't tell me people gave you money—'

'Quite a few did. Some asked what SPAN stood for and we told them. One man laughed himself silly all the way down the street, and then came back and gave us a fiver.'

Selina stared at me with a mixture of despair and admiration. 'That beats everything, it really does beat everything.'

'Well, we got over ten quid. That should be enough for paper and stamps, shouldn't it?'

'Why this sudden interest in the post, Seth?' My mother's voice was casual which always meant she was keen underneath.

'Oh, er, I've joined a sort of pen friends' club.'

'Not one of those dreadful pyramid letters where you send a pound to the first person on the list and expect to get thousands yourself?'

'No. They're rubbish.'

The phone rang, and I escaped. Alex was waiting for me on the way to school. He looked eager.

'Had any replies?'

'Nope.'

13

'It's a week since we sent out all those letters.'

'People always take a while to answer things.'

'Bet everyone just chucked our letter away.'

'Oh, belt up.' Right now, Alex got on my nerves. 'Have you remembered the maths test?'

'What maths test?'

'The one we are going to endure in about twenty minutes' time.'

'God.' Alex shrank into his blazer and followed me slowly into school. 'Oh, God.' Alexander Pigg was not so hot at maths. Nor was I, come to that.

Two letters were waiting for me when I got home. They were both a surprise.

The first one I opened was written in bright blue ink, in the sort of handwriting which looks good from a distance but is hell to read. It took me half an hour to work it out.

Dear Boys,

Thank you for your letter. I do not feel burdened by my Awful Name, so I won't join your society. Instead, I'll pass on some tips on how I've survived intact despite that burden. Your members might find them useful.

1. Long ago I decided that my name didn't matter. Stiff upper lip, grin-and-bear-it sort of thing. That's what got me through my schooldays. I pretended I didn't mind until I actually didn't mind.

2. I made myself a motto. 'Let Bottome be Top.' I said it every day. My advice is: Find a motto and live by it.

3. Make your name your fame. There's a good motto for you.

Yours etc.

Edward Bottome (Capt. rtd.)

'What does rtd. mean?' asked Alex.

'Retired.'

'So he's old.'

'Ancient.' I pictured a sea dog with a grizzled beard in a naval uniform. 'And bossy.'

'Where's the second letter?'

I dug it out of my pocket. The envelope was pink. So was the sheet Alex drew out. He looked at the signature.

'It's from a *girl*.'

It was strange, but neither of us had imagined girls would reply. They just hadn't entered into our calculations. Alex handed me the letter as if it was hot. I pushed it back at him.

'Read it, you dope. She's not going to bite you.'

Dear Seth and Alex,

Dad passed on your letter to me. I think SPAN is a *wonderful* idea. My name is Mary Peed so you can see why. I never thought of getting in touch with other people with dreadful names before. It makes me feel better already. I've asked my parents often to change their name but they can't be bothered, besides it would upset our Gran because she'd say it was being disloyal to Grandad who's dead. We could do it without her knowing, but Dad won't.

Here is my pound. (Alex looked into the envelope and fished out a postal order.) I'd love a badge, and any info on how to change my name which I will do the *moment I can*. (This was so heavily underlined she'd gone through the pink paper.) I keep thinking up good names. It's my best way of going to sleep at night.

Yours sincerely

Mary S. A. Peed (13 years)

P.S. S stands for Susan and A for Alice and I don't like either of those names much either.

P.P.S. Victimization is something I know *all* about. There are some mean people at school who think they're super clever and call me Mary Peed-in-Bed and stuff like that.

'Mary Peed-in-Bed,' repeated Alex. He started to laugh; I joined in and we laughed until we could hardly keep our bikes upright.

'Pity she's a girl,' gasped Alex. 'She doesn't sound too bad.'

I was still laughing, but I managed to get out: 'Can you imagine a roomful of people called Peed and Bottome and Smellie and Death—'

'And Bogg and Cockshut—'

'And Killjoy and Deadman—'

We got so paralytic our bikes crashed over and we ended up groaning against a wall with too much laughing. At last Alex gasped out:

'We could give a prize for the worst name.'

'If everyone had the same sense of humour.' Still weak, we sobered up and continued on our way to the bike track out at the dump.

More replies came in. One old lady called Smellie wrote and said she was sick to death of kids ringing her up and saying brilliant things like 'Are you smelly Miss Smellie' and wished she'd had the guts to change her name years ago, but now she was seventy she felt it was too late. She sent us a pound anyway and said not to bother with the badge. We got an unsigned letter, written in writing like barbed wire:

> If this is some kind of a joke, I think it is a very stupid one. I do not like receiving unsolicited letters dealing with such personal matters. Do not write to me again.

'Not bloody likely,' said Alex. 'Catch us wasting the postage.'

We had quite a few letters from boys, some quite young, nine and ten. They all wanted badges of course; I was beginning to regret the badge idea, making them was turning into a drag. In fact, I was turning out a couple one evening when the phone rang and Selina yelled up the stairs:

'Seth! Someone for you. Says he's from Midair Radio.'

Midair is our local radio station. It's funny how the whole of our house grew ears at that point. I tried to talk quietly, but the phone's in the hall and I knew they'd be listening to every word.

'Seth Slaughters? This is Harry Beckman speaking. I expect you've heard my programme *Never Say Die* on Midair? No? Well, not to worry, there's always a first time. I'm ringing you, Seth, because I saw your letter about the Society for People with Awful Names at a friend's house, and I thought it was a great idea. Very interesting. Did you think of it yourself?'

'Yes.'

'I'd like to talk to you about it, Seth. I feel there's a programme idea here somewhere. Perhaps we could meet and have a chat about it?'

'Er, yes, I don't mind—'

'Let me tell you a little more. *Never Say Die* has a slot each week for people who do unusual things, jobs, hobbies, you name it. We haven't interviewed anyone as young as you before, but that's all to the good. It'll attract the younger listeners—'

To be honest, I couldn't believe he was serious. Me on a radio programme seemed unlikely. When he met me he'd probably cool off.

'So, Seth, when can I come and see you? I suggest an early evening. I'll come to your home if you prefer, it's probably easier for the preliminary chat.'

So we fixed a day and he rang off. Rory was standing behind me; I could hear Selina moving about on the landing, ready to pounce. But Rory only wanted me to play Misfits with him.

'Not now, I've got to go out and see Alex.'

'Please, Seth. You haven't played it for ages.' He fiddled with the pack. 'Go on. Just ten minutes.'

'Listen, Rory, I absolutely promise I'll play Misfits to-morrow. For half an hour at least. Cross my heart. O.K.?'

'O.K.'

I escaped out of the front door.

Alex was over the moon. He's a radio freak, and the thought of being on it himself gave him a real buzz. He kept talking about it next day at school until I got fed up. I was afraid he'd start telling other people but he had the sense not to. Nobody at school knew about SPAN so far; and at home, only Selina. But since Harry Beckman was coming to our house to see me and Alex, I'd have to tell Mum something. She was dead curious about all the post as it was. Five minutes before Beckman was due, I said to her:

'There's a guy coming to see Alex and me. Can we use the sitting room?'

'Fine.' She wasn't really listening, she was looking at a recipe.

'I'll make some coffee for him.'

'Four ounces of butter seems a lot, Selina. Cut it down to two. And I'll need those lemons. Make what you like, Seth.'

'Is this,' said Selina, all innocent, 'the man from Midair Radio who rang up the other day?'

I could have brained her. 'Could be.'

'Midair?' Mum had woken up. 'Why is anyone from Midair coming to see Seth?'

'School play.' At that moment, the doorbell rang. I rushed to answer it, hoping it was Alex rather than Beckman. It was both of them: Beckman at the door and Alex hovering at the gate. Beckman was a podge in a revolting blue denim suit. He shook hands and I saw he even wore a gold bracelet. I got the feeling he was definitely not good news. I hurried him into the sitting room, Alex following, only to find Rory was there watching the box.

'Out.'

'Mum said I could watch this—'

'Out. Use the telly upstairs.'

'But it's black and white and crackles all the time.'

I took 50p out of my pocket, and he went without another word.

Beckman was interested in everything we said, so eager all the time I began to think he was faking it. He looked at the card index, made a few notes of his own, kept saying: 'This is very good, just what we need.' He read

19

the letters avidly, and asked if he could photocopy some of them.

'I'm not sure.' I felt uneasy. 'They may not want their names used—'

'Everyone likes being on radio.'

'I'll have to ask their permission first. I can't just let you have copies of those letters.'

He kept smiling, but I could see he was getting impatient. 'They'll make a wonderful programme—'

'You'll have to ask them first—'

'Sure, sure, Midair will do that.' His eyes returned to Mary Peed's letter, which he particularly liked. 'Most of the letters will be read by our own team, but perhaps this girl might come along for the interview? Look, here's the best solution. I'll contact her and ask her directly; she can say no if she doesn't like the idea.'

Everything was sliding out of my control. I didn't like this man Beckman, but there was Alex nodding and grinning and looking too keen by half. I felt I'd told Beckman far too much. I tried to insist that I contacted Mary Peed myself first, but he and Alex thought I was fussing. After Beckman had gone and I'd collected our SPAN stuff together, I discovered he'd nicked Mary's letter. This bothered me a lot.

I fended my family off with more lies about Beckman interviewing us about the school play. Both Alex and I are in it, so it made some sense. I told Selina the real reason. She frowned.

'Have you ever listened to *Never Say Die*?'

'No.'

'Well, I should then.'

'Why?'

'It's rubbish.'

20

She was dead right. *Never Say Die* was one of those jokey programmes with a studio audience which shrieked with laughter at the press of a switch. The idea of the programme was simple: they interviewed people who were doing something out of the ordinary, and then, after the straight interviews were over, the programme team sent the whole thing up. Laugh, laugh, laugh. So I could see exactly what Beckman was going to do; and I could also see just how the audience would fall about when the actors got going on the letters and stuff.

I'd have to stop Beckman. This couldn't happen to SPAN. People would wet themselves over a letter like Mary Peed's. Yet Beckman had said to us that the whole idea of SPAN would be presented seriously, as a social problem blah blah blah. He never went into any details about the last bit, when the fun started. I switched off his ghastly voice and sat feeling sick. I'd have to stop him doing anything at all on SPAN. I went and played Misfits with Rory.

I tried ringing him. It took thousands of phone calls before I actually caught him in his office.

'Ah, Seth. So glad you rang in. I was going to contact you. Plans for the programme are coming along nicely—'

'That's what I rang about.' There was a lot of talk going on behind Beckman. Though he talked to me as if I was the only person in the world who mattered, I got the impression he was only half-listening. 'Could you drop the idea of using SPAN? It's a lousy idea—'

'Don't worry, Seth, it'll make a great programme. You needn't get cold feet. Yes, put the letter there, Susie, I'll deal with it in a minute—'

'I haven't got cold feet. I just don't want you to do a programme on SPAN at all. Ever.'

'Come, come, Seth. Alex is very enthusiastic—and so, I have to tell you, is Mary Peed. I've just been talking to her and she's very happy to give an interview. It would disappoint them both very very much not to be on *Never Say Die*. I think you have to consider them. And we're going to end the programme this time with a phone-in, did I tell you—'

'You pinched Mary Peed's letter.'

'That was quite accidental, Seth. It just got mixed up with my papers. I'll post it straight back to you, of course. By the way, Mary sounds a sweetie, very lively and forthcoming—'

To hell with sweeties. 'So you won't consider ditching this programme?'

'Do explain why you've suddenly gone cold on the idea, dear boy. You seemed so keen the other evening.' His voice was oily, and this just about hid his irritation.

'Well, er, for one thing it'll be the wrong sort of publicity—'

'There is a saying, Seth, that any publicity is good publicity. I happen to believe in that.' The irritation was showing through. 'Of course, if you're too nervous to appear, I think we could manage without you. Alex is a co-founder after all, we'll just interview him.'

It was hopeless. Beckman had got his teeth into the idea, and that was that. And I wasn't going to let Alex blether on by himself, he'd say all the wrong things and give Beckman every lead he needed. As for Mary Peed, the thought of her going gush, gush, gush unchecked was too much. I imagined her as just the sort of girl I couldn't stand, all hair and toothy smiles. I went upstairs to my room and beat hell out of my drum kit until Mrs Sullivan next door started banging on the wall. She never can take more than half an hour.

Never Say Die went out live, and that gave me courage. At least Beckman couldn't edit what we said. So I worked out exactly what I would say.

We had to be at the studio an hour beforehand for a chat with Beckman who'd tell us the format. I'd never been inside Midair Radio, nor had Alex, so that bit was good. We arrived early, planning to have a thorough snoop around. The big reception hall was full of people rushing about looking important and busy. The doorman was dead suspicious of us, and checked with Beckman's office before he'd let us in. He then said we had to stay put until Beckman's secretary fetched us. We tried to wander about, but he told us to go and sit down. He'd have done well in the SS. So we sat down.

Nearby was a girl in school uniform, doing homework on her lap. She was wearing a badge that looked only too familiar. I could just see the red letters of SPAN. Alex and I wouldn't have been seen dead in a badge, except for that day collecting funds. I nudged him, and swung my eyes in the girl's direction.

'That must be Mary Peed,' says the lunatic out loud. I groan. The girl looks up and our cover's blown.

'Are you Seth and Alex?'

'Yeah.' She wasn't bad-looking, if you like the tidy, prefect type.

'I'm Mary. I'm so glad you've arrived. I've been sitting here feeling terrified. I wish I'd never said I'd do it.'

23

'So do I.' Suddenly the solution seemed absolutely simple. I stood up. 'We don't have to do it. Let's just go. Off. Away. Now.' She goggled at me.

'Hey.' Alex looked really bothered. 'You can't just leave Beckman with no programme—'

'He's probably got alternatives all ready.'

'Come on, Seth, you're not serious.'

'Too true I am.'

'Well, I'm staying. It's my first chance to go on radio, and I'm going to take it.' Alex folded his arms. He was red in the face. Mary Peed was looking at him and smiling. I could see she'd stay too. I sat down again.

'If Beckman's going to take the mickey out of SPAN, I'll murder him.'

'Why should he? He sounded very sympathetic—' Mary put her homework away into her no-nonsense, I'm-an-organized-girl briefcase.

'I don't trust him an inch,' I said. 'And lo, he appeareth.'

The other two stood up at once, with smiles on almost as big as Beckman's. He did his jokey I'm-putting-these-teenagers-at-their-ease routine all the way up to his office. He then told us how he'd planned out the programme, and roughly what he wanted us to say. Alex and Mary nodded their heads and were impressed; they obviously couldn't see what an arsehole Beckman was.

'Now Seth, I hope after all you're going to let us hear your views. A silent participator on a radio show isn't much use to the listeners, is he?' Grin, grin.

'Oh, I don't mind talking. Ask me what you like.'

'Good fellow. Well, the topic I'd like you to deal with is what to do about it if you have an awful name. Mary and Alex will have talked about the psychological and

24

social aspects. You can tell the audience about the practical side, changing your name, etc.'

'Fine. That suits me fine.'

'Then we'll ask for comments and questions when we throw it open for the phone-in. I'll handle that of course, with perhaps short comments from you all if it works out well. You can never tell with phone-ins. O.K.? Right.'

The actual studio was fascinating. We were put in a separate observation area, and through the glass could see Beckman smarming away as he introduced the first item on the programme. We could also hear what was going on. Through more glass beyond him were the technicians and various people attached to producing the programme. Suddenly Beckman's secretary came in and said we had five minutes, then she'd take us into the studio with Beckman. All three of us felt pretty sick at that point.

Once we were on the air, the programme went with amazing speed. In no time, it seemed, Beckman had got what he wanted out of Alex and Mary and was turning to me.

'And now finally we have Seth Slaughters who thought up the idea of SPAN in the first place. Seth is going to tell us what can be done about it. So to all my listeners—if any of you are unlucky enough to be a P.A.N., keep tuned in because there's hope for you!'

Once I managed to dispose of the large lump stuck at the back of my throat, it was easy. I told them about how to change your name. Then I added my own bit.

'But in some ways I'm beginning to think you ought

to stick to your own name after all. Make your name your fame, as one old bloke wrote to me. The worst thing that can happen to you, apart from teasing at school, is being patronized by people who think your name's good for a giggle but pretend not to. I mean just what this programme has done to Alex and Mary and me. We've been patronized to amuse you—hope you all had a good laugh.'

I'll give Beckman his due, he was a pro. His expression could have killed me, but his laughing voice joked away, defusing what I'd said and turning it to the programme's advantage. During the phone-in, which was about as naff as phone-ins usually are, he made sure he never gave me a chance to answer. His secretary showed us out pretty smartly when the programme ended.

'I was proud of you,' said Selina. 'It's time someone talked straight to those sycophantic media people.'

'I'm not sure it was worth it.' I felt depressed all the way home. Alex had gone for a coffee with Mary Peed and they were clearly not pleased with me.

'Of course it was worth it. That chap Beckman's a creep.' Selina went on and on about the programme until I began to believe her. I went off to my room and was just about to start on my drums when Selina stuck her head round the door.

'By the way, what made you recant?'

'What?'

'You were going to change your name as soon as you could, remember?'

'Well. Yeah. I probably will. I'll see when the time comes.' I clashed the high-hat a couple of times, then I grinned at her. 'But think, Selina, how boring the telephone directories would become if all those awful names just disappeared. And—' a flan on my snare drum—'it might give people a buzz to have a doctor who's a violent verb.'

The next day I got a letter from Beckman. When I saw the Midair logo I nearly didn't open it.

Dear Seth,
Thank you for taking part in *Never Say Die*. Your unexpected remarks have caused a lot of feedback. That's always a good thing—abuse keeps the programme alive.

A little fact I didn't tell you—or the listeners—is this. I myself was once a P.A.N. I was driven to changing my name as soon as I was eighteen because my school nickname was Hairy Arsehole. Try living with that one!

Wishing you all the best.

Yours sincerely

Harry . . . Piles

The French Exchange

PENELOPE LIVELY

••••

There would be the Kramers—Tony and Sue—in their
Volvo and the Brands—Kevin and Lisa—in Lisa's new
Sprite. And Dad had decided to take the Renault not the
Cortina because the hatchback would be better with the
picnic things. And the forecast was good. They would
go to this prehistoric fort or whatever, anyway it was a
hill with a view, Tony Kramer said it was a gorgeous
spot. Sue was bringing some new quiche thing she was
frightfully proud of and Lisa of course, inevitably, would
be stacked to the eyeballs with her precious home-made
sorbets. And Kevin was doing some sort of wine cup.

And oh, her mother went on, voice a notch higher,
shouting up the stairs, isn't it a shame, Nick Kramer isn't
coming after all. He's in France. On an exchange. The
Kramers have got the Exchange so they're bringing him
instead. He's your and Nick's age and he's called Jean
something. Oh well, we'll just have to be nice.

She stood in front of her mirror. She heard her mother
clatter back to the kitchen. It didn't matter about Nick
Kramer; he was duff anyway. What did matter was that
the new jeans quite definitely made her look fat. She
took them off and put on the blue skirt instead but then
the stripy T-shirt was wrong so she substituted the pink

28

embroidered top with the low neck and suddenly her collar bones looked enormous. Deformed. She'd always known there was something wrong with her collar bones, it didn't matter how much people she confidentially asked swore there wasn't. So the pink top was hopeless. That left the yellow shirt that made her look pasty, which was definitely out, so there was nothing for it but to start all over again with the jeans and the loose cream top that hid her bulge but made her bosom non-existent. And then her mother was shouting that they were here, so in despair she had to stay like that and go down, bulging and bosom-less and discontented, and say hello to them all—Sue Kramer with tight white pants and one of those great baggy shirts and Lisa Brand in a sort of pink linen jacket and skirt thing and her hair done with silver highlights.

Hello, hello, they were all saying, and her mother was wondering if the barbecue stuff should go in the Volvo not the Renault and her father was showing Kevin Brand the new ice-bucket. 'Hi there, Anna,' Sue Kramer cried. 'Jean-Paul, here's Mary and Clive Becket, and Anna, and the Brands you've already met, I say Kevin we were pursuing you all the way down the dual carriageway . . .'

He wasn't very tall and he wore glasses and had spots. Copious spots. Not even remotely good-looking. Oh well. He inclined his head neatly, five times, and said '*Bonjour.*' 'English, Jean-Paul,' scolded Sue. 'You must *try.*' And Jean-Paul said 'Good day' and inclined again. But everyone was busy now arguing about who should go in which car and her father was looking at Kevin's this year's *AA Book of the Road* with the new by-pass on it.

Eventually it was all sorted out. Jean-Paul would come in the Renault with them and the Kramers would take the barbecue stuff and follow and Kevin and Lisa would go on ahead because Lisa would want to go like the clappers once they were out of the speed limit.

He didn't say much. He got in the back beside her and said '*Pardon*' when their knees bumped, and when her mother asked where he lived in France he told her and when her father asked if he was keen on sport he said no, perfectly politely. She took a look at him, sideways, without turning her head. Poor boy—it must be awful being so spotty. She could see half her own face in the driving-mirror; the new eye shadow was good, really good. Her mother was talking about Lisa and how she'd put on weight, did you notice, Anna? And then she remembered Jean-Paul and asked if he had any brothers and sisters and Jean-Paul said yes, he had one sister younger and one brother older, Solange and Stéphan, and that rather finished that off so her mother went back to Lisa and wondered if she'd like a copy of the F-plan diet.

South London thinned out and became Surrey towns all joined on to each other and presently bits of country appeared and villages. Jean-Paul gazed out of the window. Once they passed a church and he turned, watching it recede. He said, '*C'est beau, ça.* It is of when?' 'That's a church,' said Anna's mother. 'Yes,' said Jean-Paul. 'Of what time, I ask.' 'Oh goodness,' said Anna's mother. 'I'm no good on that sort of thing.' '*Pardon*,' said Jean-Paul. He must be a Catholic, Anna thought. She looked down and saw that he had awful shoes on, not the sort of thing people wear at all, but presumably they were French. She felt a bit sorry for him. The next time he looked her way she smiled brightly, to make up for the spots and the awful shoes, and he smiled back. His smile didn't somehow go with the rest of him; it was somehow detached, as though perhaps he didn't realize about the spots, or the shoes, or the peculiar way his hair grew at the back. Oh well.

Another village. A stretch of more open country. Jean-Paul leaned forward and said, 'Excuse. I wish the toilet please.'

Anna went crimson. How ghastly. Poor thing. Having to ask. If it had been her she'd have died rather, in someone else's car, people you didn't know. Actually Jean-Paul should have died rather, in fact. Waves of embarrassment and irritation came from the back of her parents' heads. Her father said, 'Oh ... Yes ... Sure thing. Soon as there's a likely spot, right?' And after another minute he pulled in at a lay-by beside a wood and the Kramers' Volvo pulled in behind and Jean-Paul got out and plunged off into the bushes.

Anna's mother sighed. 'I ask you! I mean, you can't tell a sixteen-year-old he should have been before we started.'

Sue Kramer appeared at the window. 'Sorry. But there it is—if Nick doesn't get his French O-level he'll have to take it again next year. Jean-Paul's been awfully little trouble, actually.' And she began to talk to Anna's mother about the holiday the Kramers were going to have in Portugal and presently Jean-Paul came out of the wood and got into the car and Sue went back to the Volvo and they all set off again.

Anna's cheeks still flamed. She slid a glance at Jean-Paul. He didn't, actually, seem embarrassed at all. He was looking out of the window and when they went

31

through a place with a market square with old-looking houses he opened his mouth as though about to say something and then shut it again and smiled slightly, but to himself. Anna's cheeks went back to normal and she thought about their own holiday which would be in Greece and the awful problem was would she or would she not have lost five pounds by then and be able to feel absolutely all right in a bikini or would she have to spend all of every day on the beach holding her tummy in. None of the barbecue today, definitely none, and only a sliver of Sue Kramer's quiche.

Jean-Paul was saying something. She abandoned the bikini problem. 'Sorry?'

'I say, you should wear a hat of fur. Pretty—with black hair.' He gestured, circling her head, an odd, rather stylish gesture.

'A hat?' She stared, perplexed. Actually, her hair was very dark brown, not black.

'Karenina. Anna. For your name.'

'Oh.' She saw now; there was some Russian novel, the film had been on the telly once. 'Well . . . ' She laughed, awkwardly. 'It would be a bit hot, on a day like this.'

Jean-Paul looked at her attentively, and then shrugged. '*Tant pis.*' He gazed once more out of the window.

And now they were turning off on to the B road that would take them to this hill and her mother was saying let's pray the charcoal lights properly, I felt such a fool last time with the Kramers, and oh God did I put the avocado dip in? Down lanes and through a village and round a corner and there was the red Sprite parked on the verge and the Brands sitting beside it on folding chairs like film directors use with LISA and KEVIN stencilled on the backs in big black letters.

There was a lot of shunting of cars to and fro to get them off the road and then a lot of unpacking and arranging of who would carry what and in the middle of it Anna's mother suddenly shrieked and pointed at the front of the Kramers' car.

'Tony! You got it! And we never even noticed!'

So everyone looked and now Anna too saw the number-plate: AJK 45.

'Oh, neat!' said Lisa. 'Your age too. I'm green with envy.'

'How much did that set you back?' asked Anna's father, and Tony Kramer grinned and said he wasn't telling. Jean-Paul was looking at Tony in a most odd way; he wasn't smiling but you felt he was somehow laughing. Everyone began to fuss round the picnic things and the folding chairs and the barbecue again and Jean-Paul said to Anna, 'Why?'

'Why what?'

He pointed at the number-plate.

He must be a bit slow on the uptake, she thought. 'It's his initials. And his age.'

'I know,' said Jean-Paul. 'But why?'

She couldn't think, when it came down to it. 'Well, it's a thing people do. There are lists in newspapers. Some of them are terribly expensive.' Actually her parents had been looking for ages for MRB or CTB but for some reason she decided not to say so. Jean-Paul gazed thoughtfully at Tony Kramer and said, *'Curieux.'*

'You're supposed to talk English,' said Anna sternly. He was four months younger than her, it had emerged.

'D'accord,' said Jean-Paul, and grinned. Really, his spots were the worst she'd ever seen.

There was a fuss going on now because Lisa had

33

discovered she'd forgotten her sun-tan lotion and although Sue and Anna's mother had some they were the wrong kinds apparently, Lisa had to use this special one, but eventually she decided she might be able to manage with a hat. They set off, through the gate and up the hill along a rough track.

Everyone was carrying something: the men quite loaded with chairs and loungers and barbecue equipment, the women more lightly burdened with picnic hampers and coolers and ice-buckets. Anna and Jean-Paul were at the back of the procession. Anna had her mother's basket with paper napkins and plastic cutlery and garlic bread in foil; Jean-Paul bore the bag of barbecue charcoal and Kevin Brand's wicker wine-bottle carrier with four bottles wrapped in tissue paper. He padded along a couple of paces behind her; the rest of them snaked ahead, calling out to each other, Lisa slipping and sliding on high-heeled sandals.

Jean-Paul said, 'Very serious—*la pique-nique*.'

She turned to look at him. Was he laughing? No, his expression was perfectly solemn. But something about his voice ... Anna stared ahead at her laden parents, and their laden friends, at the glitter of chrome and the bright glow of plastic. She said—attack and defence together—'Don't your parents do this kind of thing?'

'Ah yes. Absolutely. Also very serious.'

She felt, now, faintly uncomfortable. It was as though you were playing a game with someone that you knew was much worse at it than you, and suddenly they started doing things they shouldn't be able to.

'You enjoy yourself?' enquired Jean-Paul.

'Of course,' said Anna firmly. After a moment she added, 'Aren't you?'

34

'*Bien sûr*,' said Jean-Paul. He was, she saw, grinning hugely. He waved a hand at the landscape—'It is beautiful day. The sun shines. All is agreeable.'

The track had petered out and they were walking on close-cropped turf up the hillside, which rose ahead of them in a series of bumpy terraces on which sheep grazed and small bright flowers grew. The leading group—Kevin and Lisa and Anna's father—had come to a halt and as the others caught up with them an argument arose about the appropriate point at which to pitch camp. Anna's mother wanted to stop further on, at that flat place; Lisa wanted to be near a tree in case she needed some shade. Everyone disputed. Lisa said, 'Oh never mind me, I'll manage somehow, at a pinch I can go back to the car,' and Tony Kramer said, 'Oh no, we're not having that, love. Right, then, the tree has it.' Kevin gave him a look that was sort of not quite as friendly as it might be and Anna's parents were telling each other that they needn't be so bossy in that joke-tone that, Anna knew, could topple over into not joking at all. And Sue Kramer wasn't joining in but gazed into the distance and tapped one toe on the grass.

Jean-Paul said to Anna, 'They enjoy themself too, do you think?' Anna, ruffled, pretended to be doing up her sandal. She was sweating after the climb and suddenly had the most ghastly feeling she might have forgotten to use any deodorant.

A decision, eventually, was made. Chairs, loungers, barbecue were disposed upon the bright grass. Lisa had loosened the heel of her shoe and Tony Kramer was trying to fix it with his natty miniature pliers on a key-chain and Sue Kramer was wishing loudly he'd get on with the wine cup—everyone must be parched. Kevin was setting up the barbecue, in silence. Anna's mother was speaking to Anna's father in that bright, high voice that meant trouble.

The barbecue was lit. The wine cup was made. Kebabs sizzled. Sue Kramer arranged herself on a lounger, gazed skywards and said, 'Bliss!' Glasses were filled. Birds sang. The spare ribs and the chicken joined the kebabs. Glasses were re-filled. Anna's mother uttered an awful cry—'Oh Christ, I've left the second barbecue sauce at home in the fridge!'

'Oh, for heaven's sake . . . ' said Anna's father.

There was a silence. 'But there's this delicious-looking one over here,' said Sue Kramer.

'But just the one!' cried Anna's mother. 'There should be a choice!'

'We'll manage,' said Kevin Brand. 'Forget it.'

'*Quel horreur* . . . ' said Jean-Paul, to the grass, shaking his head.

And now the kebabs were handed round on the gay paper plates, and the spare ribs and the chicken and the one sauce and the bright serviettes, two apiece—for lips and lap. And everyone was saying how brilliant of Tony to know about this gorgeous place.

'We are in the middle of a . . . what is it? . . . a field of battle?' asked Jean-Paul.

They all stared at him. 'Some sort of camp, I think,' said Tony. 'Prehistoric.'

'Or thereabouts,' said Lisa. There was general laughter. 'Now, now,' said Tony. 'It's not nice to make fun of other people's ignorance.' Lisa pulled a face at him and he aimed a spare rib at her, threateningly. 'Don't you dare!' cried Lisa. 'These pants are sheer hell to wash, I'll have you know.'

36

Jean-Paul watched, without expression. He turned to Anna and remarked, quietly, 'There is a tradition, then, of picnic here.'

'I suppose so,' muttered Anna. She had this feeling that everything was getting out of control – not least, in some odd way, Jean-Paul. There he was, with his spots and his awful shoes, and six months younger than her, and yet you had this peculiar sense of him being somehow much older and floating above and beyond the spots and the shoes. She stroked her armpit, surreptitiously; she was sure there were visible sweat-marks on the cream top.

The quiche was being handed round now, and the salad, and the garlic bread, and more wine cup. Everyone was talking at once and Lisa Brand was shouting rather and Kevin was having an argument with Tony Kramer about something to do with the insides of cars, whether Tony's Volvo had a this or a that. Jean-Paul said to Anna, 'You interest in cars?'

'Not really,' said Anna, after a moment's hesitation.

'Moi non plus,' said Jean-Paul.

And now they were moving on to the dessert: the mousse and the sorbet and the little biscuity things Sue Kramer had brought. A different lot of gay paper plates; more bright plastic cutlery. There was debris all around now: heaps of plastic and paper and left-over food and bottles and glasses. A little way off a small posse of sheep stood gazing and chewing. 'Don't look now,' said Lisa. 'But we're being watched.' Tony Kramer laughed uproariously.

Anna glanced at Jean-Paul, but not so that he would notice. He was looking at some little orange butterflies that danced above the turf, and then his attention switched to a bird that hung in the sky just above the brow of the hill, its wings quivering. And then, as Kevin circulated again with the wine cup and a few drops got spilled on Lisa's white pants, causing distress, he observed that, in just the same grave and attentive way as he watched the butterflies and the bird.

The chatter decreased. Lisa was still dabbing at her pants, scowling. Kevin had wandered off a little distance and was lying on his back on the grass. Anna's mother was saying that of course it was heavenly here but what would be nice now would be a swim.

Jean-Paul rose, stowed his dirty plate, cutlery and napkin neatly in Anna's mother's basket and strolled away over the grass. He squatted down beside a clump of flowers.

Sue Kramer said to Anna, 'You are being so frightfully good with him. I'm afraid he's rather a dull boy, but there it is. Anyway, you're sweet.'

Anna smiled, embarrassed. Actually she'd never been entirely sure she liked Sue Kramer. Nick Kramer she'd known since he was about three, and he was absolutely hopeless.

'And the acne . . . ' said Lisa. 'One wants to simply pick them up and plunge them in some enormous vat of disinfectant, boys of that age.'

Anna looked towards Jean-Paul who, at that moment, glanced over his shoulder, caught her eye and waved. 'Look . . . ' he called.

'Be nice, darling,' said Anna's mother.

There was a glinting coppery butterfly sitting on a plant, opening and closing its wings. Jean-Paul pointed, without speaking. Anna was at a loss; it was a bit odd, to put it bluntly, for a boy to be going on about a butterfly.

'A butterfly,' she said, with slight desperation.

'Yes,' said Jean-Paul. 'Of what kind?'

'I've no idea.'

'You are not interest in nature, either?'

'Well, quite,' said Anna (blushing now, curse it).

'I am interest,' said Jean-Paul, 'in astronomy, philosophy and the music of Mozart.'

Anna went rigid. Thanks heavens at least the others hadn't heard him; they'd have died laughing. He was perfectly serious, that was the awful thing. What on earth could one say? He was gazing at her, reflectively.

'Tell me,' he went on, 'why did your parents embarrass? About I need to go to the toilet from the car.'

She didn't know where to look. 'I don't know,' she muttered.

Jean-Paul laughed. 'Perhaps they are people who do not need to go to the toilet, never. *Formidable!*'

She looked back to the picnic group. Kevin Brand was still lying on the grass. Her parents were tidying up. Sue Kramer was sitting a little apart, reading a magazine. Lisa Brand and Tony Kramer were walking up the hill together; you could hear them laughing.

'I'm sorry,' said Jean-Paul. 'Now I make you embarrass too. I am not very nice. Shall we go for a walk?'

'All right,' said Anna. In the car, she remembered, she had smiled brilliantly at him to make up for his spots and his shoes.

They went round the flank of the hill, along the crest of one of the great ridges that lapped it. And Jean-Paul, incredibly, began to sing. She was afraid the others might hear. He sang this cheerful little song, the words of which she could not quite catch, and when they got to a point from which you could see great blue distances of landscape all around he stopped and waved at it and said, '*Pas mal, alors?*' He was, she saw, perfectly happy.

She stared at him in surprise. There he was, this not at all nice-looking boy who wasn't tall enough, spending the day with lots of people he didn't know, most of whom hadn't spoken a word to him, and he was happy. It was ridiculous, really.

She said, 'Do you like staying with the Kramers?'

Jean-Paul shrugged. '*Ça va.* They are very kind. I must learn English for my examination.'

'Like Nick's got to get his French O-level.'

He grinned. 'So everybody inconveniences themself a little.'

They had reached the brow of the hill. Below them on one side was the picnic site, with Anna's parents and Kevin and Sue Kramer and Lisa. Lisa's laugh floated up to them. And then suddenly she was flapping her hands around her head and there was a shriek and Tony was flapping his hands too and bending over her.

'*La pauvre dame,*' said Jean-Paul. 'She is bit, I think. A—how do you say it—*une guêpe.*'

'Wasp,' said Anna. She didn't feel all that sorry for Lisa Brand. Actually she thought Lisa had been going on rather, with her precious white pants and her jokes. Lisa and Tony were starting back up the hill now, Lisa with her hand clasped to her shoulder.

'Do you believe in God?' said Jean-Paul.

She looked at him in horror. 'I don't know.'

'*Moi—non.* Not since I am twelve years old. Because of he makes everything beautiful and then puts in the middle a wasp. Everything is nice and then—pouff!—a bus come and run over your mother.'

'Honestly?' said Anna, shocked.

'*Pas actuellement*. But it is what happen. *La souffrance*. So I do not think there can be anyone who make a world like that, or if there is he is bad and he is not God, because God is good. *Pas vrai?*'

Quite frankly, she'd never heard anyone talk like that in her life. You didn't know whether to laugh, or what. I mean, sitting on a hill talking about God. But there he was, doing it as though it were the most normal thing in the world.

Lisa and Tony passed them. Lisa was leaning on Tony's arm, still clutching her shoulder. Tony waved and Lisa smiled bravely. Jean-Paul said, 'Perhaps that lady does not suffer so terrible. In the Middle Age people are roasting each other on fires and putting in hot oil.'

'Don't,' said Anna. She was hopeless at history, anyway; it was her worst subject, except maths. And this conversation was quite beyond her, out of control like everything on this stupid picnic. For two pins she'd have gone back to the others, except that in some peculiar way it had now become Jean-Paul who made decisions, not her. Just as, eerily, it was Jean-Paul who seemed at ease in this place, on this hill-side in a foreign country, rather than the rest of them.

He said, 'When I will be president of the Republic— no, when I will be king—king is more amusing, *tant pis pour la Révolution*—when I will be king there will be no earthquakes and no bad weather and I will give to everyone discs of the music of Mozart.' He looked at Anna. 'And what will you make, when you are queen?'

It was silly, this, really—I mean if any of one's friends could hear . . . 'No more maths.'

'Ah. That is difficult for the banks and the shops and the men of business. Never mind, we arrange.'

41

She didn't know if she liked him or not. But more disconcerting was the fact that, so far as he was concerned, it quite evidently didn't matter. He wasn't bothered, one way or the other. And, maddeningly, it began to matter what he thought of her. Which was absurd . . . a boy like that. She tried to think of something to say that would be funny, or clever; nothing came.

'So that's where you've got to.' Her mother appeared suddenly behind them. 'Lisa's been stung by a wasp. The most unnecessary commotion, frankly. Tony's gone off to that village we came through to get some antihistamine. And someone left the top off the ice-bucket— wouldn't you know—so I can't do the iced tea.' She looked round irritably. 'I said all along we should have gone to a beach.'

'Where's Dad?'

'He's got one of his headaches, rather predictably. So Sue and I have been clearing up entirely on our own. Kevin's gone off in a huff.' She remembered Jean-Paul and said brightly, 'I'm so glad Anna's been looking after you.' She gave Anna a conspiratorial glance of sympathy. 'Anyway, I thought I'd better start rounding people up.'

They walked down the hill. Anna's mother told Jean-Paul that this was a frightfully pretty part of the country and Jean-Paul nodded politely and Anna's mother glanced at his shoes and his haircut and Anna knew what she was thinking. She wished she was someone else. She wished, particularly, that Jean-Paul was somewhere else but for her own sake rather than for his.

They reached the picnic place, where Anna's father, Lisa Brand, Kevin Brand and Sue Kramer were all sitting a little apart from each other and not saying anything. Lisa was holding a handkerchief to her neck and Anna's father had his eyes closed. And then Tony Kramer came panting up the hill waving a tube and Lisa cried, 'Oh, Tony, bless you—you really are an angel.' Kevin Brand picked up a newspaper and began to read it and Sue Kramer said, 'Sir Lancelot to the rescue,' and laughed in a not particularly amused way.

Anna's mother had just discovered she had trodden in a pile of sheep-muck and was hopping about with one of her new Russell & Bromley sandals off, trying to clean it.

Jean-Paul looked around at them all. He smiled benignly. He said, 'I wish to thank for you bring me to this charming place.' They all gazed at him in astonishment and he continued to smile benignly and sat down on the grass. 'I enjoy myself very much,' he said.

For a moment there was silence. Then Tony Kramer exclaimed heartily, 'And that goes for everyone, I imagine. Terrific outing. Sort of day that should go on for ever.'

'Absolutely,' murmured Lisa.

'Quite,' said Anna's father. 'Though alas we, I'm afraid, will have to push off shortly.' He gave Anna's mother one of those looks that was not a look but an instruction and she scowled back and continued to rearrange picnic baskets and barbecue stuff.

They walked in procession down the hill. This time Jean-Paul led the way and was the most heavily burdened, having insisted on carrying the two loungers. Even so, he walked faster than anyone else; he was, Anna could hear, singing that little song again. No one else was saying much except Lisa who was telling Tony Kramer her neck felt heaps better now, entirely thanks to him.

The right possessions were stowed into the right cars. They told each other what a marvellous day it had been. Anna's mother kissed everyone and Sue Kramer kissed everyone except Lisa Brand and Jean-Paul went round shaking hands. When he got to Anna he said, 'When I am king I make you my Minister of Finance, O.K.?' and Anna went scarlet. Jean-Paul got in with the Kramers and Kevin and Lisa got into their Sprite and Anna got into the Renault with her parents. Engines started. Everyone waved.

Anna's mother said, 'What on earth was that boy saying?'

'Nothing.'

'Did you manage to find something to talk to him about?'

'Sort of,' said Anna distantly.

There was a grass-stain on her new jeans and she had eaten not one small slice of quiche but two helpings of everything so she would have put on about three pounds. But all that was the least of it.

They travelled back along the same roads but she did not feel the same at all. Ahead of them was the Kramers' car and through the rear window she could see Jean-Paul's head, and that too was different, uncomfortably different; it spoke now not of spots and a ghastly haircut but of small coppery butterflies and conversation that embarrassed, that left you uncertain, as though you had peered through strange windows. Jean-Paul did not turn round and presently the Volvo was lost in traffic.

King

JON BLAKE

●●●●

For this story to make any sense, you've got to understand what Simon Waites was like. Thing is, Waitesy never *ever* done nothing wrong. If the lot of us wagged Worzel's lesson, he'd still go on his own. And if we all had Harjit thinking the Head was after him, Waitesy'd let on without a *second thought*.

I don't suppose it's hard to guess how a youth like that got on in our school. He joined just about every club out so he never had to go in the playground. Mummy and Daddy picked him up straight after school, and no one ever saw him till next morning. Half past eight he'd be in, with his little black briefcase full of homework. They must've cropped a forest to find that youth enough paper.

Funny enough though, not all the teachers liked him. They liked the fact he never answered back all right, but they weren't so keen on him following them all about, like a little dog. Hung on every little word they said, he did. Like it was a matter of *life and death*. All a teacher had to do was cough, and he'd try and write it down.

Of course, you don't get the full picture till you know what he looked like. Well, put it this way. If you stuck a pair of wings on him, all he needed was the harp and

45

the little cloud to float around on. He had these two little pudgy cheeks, and this insy red blob of a mouth like a squashed raspberry. Then there was his hair, which was all soft and curly and blonde, like a baby's. Not to mention the legs. PE was nothing without seeing his puny Dulux White sticks. Tarzan, Mr McHugh called him.

There was one weird thing about Waitesy, though. He always wore this tiny badge on his jacket, so tiny it looked like he'd just got a bad spot of dandruff. 'Elvis is King' it said, with a weeny picture of Elvis Presley before he got fat. I can't look at that badge now without remembering what happened.

It was a Friday afternoon. Worst lesson of the week—music. Old Crehan was still in the staff room having a fag as usual, while we sat round and got bored. It had been a real rubbish day, and we were just about ready for a laugh. The cupboards were all locked of course, but big Newt found a pair of drumsticks on the floor. He did a roll round some of the girls' heads, which got them really mad. Then Carlo, that half-caste youth, took over.

'Right,' he says. 'Who's gonna do us a solo, then?'

He pulls up a pair of stools and the teacher's chair.

'Heeyar, someone,' he goes. 'We got a kit.'

'What 'bout Angel Delight?' shouts Denise. ' 'E's got some drums!'

'What? 'Ow d'you know?'

'Ask 'im.'

Everyone turns on Simon.

'You know 'ow to drum?' goes Carlo. 'Got a kit, 'ave yer?'

46

We can't believe it—Simon nods! Next thing he knows, he's got the sticks in his hands.

Carlo pushes him down into a chair. 'Giz a solo then,' he says.

Simon looks at the door.

'Chicken!' goes Carlo. 'Crehan ain't comin'—we can see 'im in the staff room! Now—do it!'

Simon's stuck. He's scared to drum, and he's just as scared to back out. His babsy cheeks come up all pink at the edges. Then some of the lads put on the pressure. The second he feels the knuckles in his back, Simon panics. He starts hitting down on the stools—one, two, one, two. Some of the others start stamping out the beat with him. He hits harder, one stick to a stool, like a battery toy. Soon, everybody's joining in—stamping, clapping, you name it. And you know what? Old Angel Delight actually starts getting into it. Them sticks of his are clattering off in all directions. And the more he gets into it, the more the others drive him on. Like the lost tribe of Africa, it is. Steve and Gray are limboing under a board ruler, little Mike's doing a war dance, and even Nicki and Maria are jiggering about.

Simon's face! Would you credit it? He's got his teeth all grit together, and his eyes staring off into space, really mad and wild. You can't follow his arms, they're going that fast. The stools are near on bouncing up and down with the smacking they're getting. And know what happens next? Waitesy's red blob comes apart and—no joking—he screams. Screams! I'd never heard a racket like it. And nor had Mr Crehan.

It was Louise saw him first. She snapped straight down into her seat, and the rest of us weren't long following. All except Simon, that is. He was still battering away in

47

a world of his own. Took him at least half a minute to realize he was on his tod. He give his head three big shakes, like he was trying to get rid of something in his hair. Then he looked round and saw Crehan. The sticks dropped clean out of his hands.

That fag hadn't calmed old Crehan down much. His hands were shaking like anything as he carted Waitesy out the door. We went home at four still not knowing what had happened to him.

Carlo Hall was always one for sound ideas. It was Carlo that set up the art room door so it fell off its hinges when old Ryder went to open it. And it was Carlo that come up with the plan for Angel Delight, the morning after his little drumming solo.

'Listen,' he goes. 'Let's make out we all think Simon's dead brilliant. Like we've all changed our minds about him since we heard him drum. You know—all go quiet when he comes in the room and that.'

'Yeah!' says Lisa. 'An' we can get one o' the girls to say she wants to go out wiv 'im!'

'Sound!'

'Smart!'

'Look out—'ere 'e comes!'

The class breaks up, and pretends to be chatting about TV and that. It's hard to keep a straight face though, seeing this mousey drip sneaking in with his big posh briefcase.

Carlo edges up to him. ' 'Ere!' he says. 'What 'appened to you yesterday, then?'

Simon's blob twitches. 'Had to see Mr Wilson,' he squeaks.

'Mr *Wilson*!' goes Carlo. 'That's *trouble*, innit?'

'He gave me a warning. That was all.'

'That was all? That was all? A warning off Wilson ain't no *joke*, mate! Still . . . I bet you 'ad 'im a bit scared, dintcha?'

Simon comes over all confused. He edges back, and starts picking away at his briefcase.

'He told me next time, I'd be in for . . .'

'Yeah? Yeah? What?'

' . . . the high jump.'

Carlo looks at Newt. Newt looks at Carlo. They shake their heads.

'That's it then,' says Newt. 'You got 'im worried, aintcha?'

Simon picks harder. 'Mr Wilson wasn't worried at all,' he says.

Carlo can't believe it. 'You're *jokin'*!' he goes. 'After what old Crehan saw of you yesterday? That's why they're threatenin' yer, mate! They know what you can do!'

Lisa moves in. 'Yeah,' she says, all dreamy like. 'You got somefin you know, Simon. Somefin . . . *wild*!'

Simon flushes up red as a beetroot. Lisa giggles. Carlo shushes the rest of us. Then Denise pipes up.

'Cathy wants to go out wiv you, Simon.'

Cathy Leavis bolts for the door. We've already got it covered.

'Don't worry,' says Denise. 'She's just a bit shy. Int yer, Cath?'

Cathy shakes her fist at Denise. Simon's too keen on his own feet to notice anything.

'Well?' goes Carlo.

'What?' squeaks Simon.

'You gonna make 'er an 'appy woman?'

49

'No.'

Carlo nods, dead slow. 'We'll see,' he says. 'Anyhow—when's the next show, then?'

Simon's head jitters from side to side. 'Get in trouble,' he says.

'Rubbish!' goes Carlo. 'You ain't scared o' what Wilson said, are yer? Listen, mate—you're a star round 'ere now. You get in trouble, an' you got the *whole school* behind yer.'

Simon can't stop a little smile creeping out.

'Sound!' goes Newt, squeezing his big hands together. 'We'll fix yer up wiv a kit.'

'What 'bout down Smokers' Corner?' says Denise.

'Great idea,' says Newt. 'No one'll know if we stick some boxes an' stuff over there.'

Carlo lays a hand on Simon's shoulder. 'What you say, mate?' he goes. 'Won't get into no trouble over there, will yer?'

Simon shrugs.

'Smart!' says Newt. 'This lunchtime, right?'

Carlo cheers, and the rest join in with it. Simon's surrounded by people slapping him on the back.

'Eh,' says Carlo, tapping Simon's Elvis badge. 'Long live the King, eh?'

'Long live the King!' everyone yells, just like that.

Of course, it wouldn't have worked if we hadn't planned it proper. For a start, everyone we knew had to be in on the joke. It wasn't no good a dozen of us cheering if everyone else was laughing their heads off at Simon. Next, we had to make sure Cathy'd play the game. Wasn't asking for much. If anyone asked her if she really fancied Simon, all she had to do was shut up and not deny it. Even so, Cathy hates getting shown up, and in the end it come down to bribery. Five p. from everyone in class to pretend to have a crush on Simon.

So there we were, that lunchtime, trooping across the school field to Smokers' Corner. Some were carrying orange boxes, some had bust-up chairs, and a couple brought bin lids—for cymbals, like. Hanson was on duty, which was great, seeing as he always pretended to be blind anyhow. I'll tell you what though. He must've been deaf and all if he couldn't hear the racket that come out of that copse. Simon on his own was bad enough, but what with thirty odd kids shouting along, you half expected the trees to come crashing down round us.

There was no doubt about it. Simon was starting to like the attention. He even stopped a couple of times, to tell us things like 'This is the beat from *All Shook Up*.' After a bit, we weren't just making jungle noises. We were chanting out 'King! King! King!', driving him on to hit that pile of rubbish harder and harder. When he took a rest, we even got Denise and Sonia to mop his face with a little towel. He didn't even flinch—just looked dead serious and moody, like James Dean. Cath pretended to get dead jealous, and had to be tugged away from Denise. Not even the bell could stop old Angel Delight now. He got into English five minutes late, all flushed and sweaty. When Lanky Binney asked him to explain himself, Simon just did a big shrug, sat down, and clicked all the joints in his fingers. Binney couldn't believe it! He had Simon out front, straightening his shirt and apologizing. All the while though, the King's got this great stupid grin across his face. 'Good stuff, King,' Carlo says to him when he sits down again.

What I'd have give to have seen that staff room next

morning. All them teachers rushing around talking about Simon, like ants with their nest kicked over. I mean, the end of the world can't have been far off if Simon Waites had *actually been naughty*!

You could tell how rattled they were, the way they started jumping on any little thing he done wrong. Funny enough, it was the worst thing they could've done. Simon got it into his head that he was a real dangerous rebel now, and we made sure the idea stuck. The lessons got worse, and the drumming solos got better. After a few days, he wasn't going red no more when someone said 'Hi, King' to him. After a week, he was nodding back.

Then there was Cathy. She earned her money, I'll give her that. Most of the time, she'd just be gazing at him, in the distance like. Now and then, though, she'd carry his sticks for him, or ask for help with her homework. And when a third year started asking if Simon was a boy or a girl, Cath shouted out, ' 'E's more of a man than you'll ever be!' We give her an extra ten p. for that.

The King got used to having Cathy around. One lunchtime, he even asked her for a towel. Next day, he asked her for a microphone.

It was weird, that day. The King had started off more or less as normal, but after ten minutes, he had this real *confused* look on him. Suddenly, he stops drumming, and points out with his stick.

'Giz that mike!' he says.

It's Cath he's staring at. She looks blank.

'The *mike*!' he goes again. 'Giz the *mike*, will yer?'

All Cath's got on her's a pencil case. Then we realize it's *that* Simon's after. A real eerie feeling comes over everyone. Simon stretches out and grabs the case. He holds it up to his mouth.

'One for the money . . . two for the show . . . three to get ready, then GO MAN GO!'

The King jumps clean off his stool, twists his little arse, and launches into this mad screeching song. Looks like he's been kicked where it hurts.

'You can do anythin' . . . but *lay offa my blue suede shoes*!'

The King kicks up one of his Hush Puppies, and falls over. Newt turns to me with his mouth hanging open.

'He's cracked,' he says.

I look round. Nothing but open mouths. They watch the King get up again, and try to twist with some girl. A couple of fourth years decide they've seen enough. One of them snatches the pencil case. 'Give it back!' yells Simon. There's a mass of swinging arms, dead vicious. Somehow the King gets smacked in the face and winds up on his arse. The pencil case and the fourth years disappear. Cath's crying, and bawling out 'Where's my case?'

Evil it is, dead evil. The crowd hang around, but don't do nothing to help Simon up. It's only when they start to break up that Carlo comes to his senses.

'King!' he goes, rushing up to him. 'You O.K., King?'

Simon props himself up and rubs his jaw. 'That kid's *dead*,' he says.

'Just say the word,' says Carlo. 'We're your mates, remember?'

Simon nods, then frowns. 'It's more than mates I need,' he says. 'It's bodyguards.'

Next day, the King wasn't seen nowhere without Newt and Carlo on each side.

The shows couldn't last forever. Sure enough, one day

old Binney himself's on duty. With the help of a few creeps from the fifth year, he turfs the whole scene out of Smokers' Corner. The drum kit's taken to bits and carried back to where it come from.

As it happened, it was just as well. The joke was wearing thin, and we'd run out of new ideas. Once the shows had been banned though, everyone was dying to see another. What was more, the King was really in deep now—on report, threats to have his old dears in, you name it. First division at last.

The next step was a secret concert—a real big one. We decided on the school pavilion, after school the next Friday. News was put out over our pirate radio station (Carlo's CB)—along with a live interview with the King. Really loved that, Simon did. Told us all how he used to earn the family's living by singing in the subways. Explained how people used to hate him when he was holding himself back, but now pay good money for a lock of his hair.

'Is it true you go out with Cathy Leavis?' someone asks him.

Simon puts down the CB and looks at Cathy. 'Is it?' he goes.

'You askin'?' she says, to a massive 'Ooo' all round.

'Talk about it after school,' says the King. He tries to stay cool, but it don't quite come off. He's near on wetting himself with excitement, actually asking a girl out.

'You gonna sing us somefin then?' someone asks.

The King reaches out, dead lazy. 'Giz a mike,' he goes.

We have a look around. Newt finds a bust-off chair leg. Simon takes hold of it, and he's away. *Jailhouse Rock* this one is.

Everyone seems to be in on it now. First years, fifth years, even Terry the caretaker. All laughing their heads off. Simon can hear them all right, but he thinks they're laughing *with* him, not *at* him. He even tries to put some comic bits in his routine. People are laughing straight into his face, and he's loving every minute. He drops on to the floor and wriggles about like a beetle. Feet stab out and kick him in the leg. He never even notices.

A bunch of girls at the back are getting stroppy.

'Someone should stop him,' goes Lynn Barlow.

'It ain't funny no more,' says Sonia Stevens. 'It's pathetic.'

Some first year girl with freckles turns round. 'What you on about?' she says.

'That,' says Sonia, pointing at Simon. 'It's cruel.'

'What is? I don't get yer.'

'Laughin' at 'im, that's what.'

'*Who's* laughing at 'im?'

'What you on about? They *all* are, ain't they?'

'Laughin' at Simon Waites? Why?'

'What yer mean, "why"?'

'Well, 'e's all right, int 'e?'

'All right? *Simon*?'

'Good drummer, ain' 'e? An' 'e don' 'alf give teachers some stick.'

Sonia turns right round to the first year, hands on hips. 'No, stupid,' she goes. 'It's a *joke*, right? All this about 'im bein' the King, an' everyone 'ero-worshippin' 'im! Simon Waites is a *prannet*!'

This first year looks right put out. 'Well that's what *you* think,' she says. 'But I wouldn't go spreadin' it round his first year fan club.'

Carlo was having nothing of it. 'Puh!' he says to Sonia. 'You been taken for a ride, woman.'

'Well she was a bloody good actress, then,' says Sonia.

'Come off it,' says Carlo. 'Even *you* couldn't fancy Simon Waites. He's the piddliest runt in school!'

'Why don't yer ask someone yerself?'

'I will!'

Carlo looks around the lower school library. Then he pounces on some little black girl.

'You 'eard o' Simon Waites?' he goes.

'Why? You a mate of 'is?'

'Might be.'

The girl yanks herself free and races over to her pals. 'See 'im?' she goes. ''E knows *Simon Waites*!'

Carlo don't know what's hit him. All round him they are, like wasps at a jam pot. Fix us a date, get us a photo, bring us a stick.

'Leave off, will yer?' goes Carlo. 'This a joke, or what?'

'What yer mean?' goes this stumpy blonde girl. ''E's *lovely*. 'E's so *sweet*.'

'Yeah,' says another. 'An' sexy.'

That's enough for Carlo. He's legging it for all he's worth. Mind you, it still takes him a good five minutes to shake them.

Of course, the whole thing could still be a set-up. Playing us at our own game, like. Thing was though, once you actually got talking to a few people round school, it looked less and less like a joke. The suckers really were swallowing it! Every time Simon give another teacher some lip, seemed there was another dozen kids wanting to be his mate. Cath was starting to get the evil eye off other girls, and even a couple of poison pen letters. We half expected her to back out, but funny

56

enough, she seemed keener than ever to play the game. With that many girls wanting to go out with Simon, he was starting to look like a dead good thing.

Something had to be done, and fast. We decided to fix the secret concert. We'd rig it so that none of the King's real fans would get to see it—only the people laughing at him. We'd let him do his little act as normal, except there wouldn't be no shouting along, and no clapping at the end. Just dead stone-cold silence. Sixty odd kids, all silent, and staring at him. Then there'd be a signal, and we'd start up the slow handclap. After that, the chant. And just to make sure he'd really got the message, every one'd pick up a little stone, and chuck it at him. Then a bigger one. Then a bigger one still. When he yelled for his bodyguards, Newt and Carlo'd shake their heads, and chuck stones themselves. 'The King is dead,' they'd say.

It was a race against time. Two days before the concert, Simon went and led a crowd of kids down to the local chippy, after the bloke had refused to serve some nipper. More trouble for the King at school, and more trouble for us making sure the tickets went to the right people.

Then Simon got smacked again. A third year this time—that skinhead, Mike O'Grady. His girlfriend had said she fancied the King. Mike thought she ought to know what the King was made of. Whether his blood was really blue, like. We found him behind the bins. He was clutching at his guts, with a mess all over his nose.

'Where was yer?' he whines, when he sees Newt.

Cathy and Denise come rushing round the corner. Cath's face drops. She's near on crying at the sight of the King. While we're trying to keep a straight face, she dabs at his nose with a hankie.

'You O.K., Simon?' she goes.

'Fine,' he goes, tears plopping out both eyes.

Cath looks round. 'What you gawpin' at?' she says. 'Ain't yer got nuffin better to do?'

'Just seein' what's up, ain't we?' goes Newt.

'Well ain't yer seen enough yet? Someone's 'it 'im, that's what! An' 'e ain't done *nuffin* to them! You make me *sick*, you boys! All got to be little 'ard men, aintcha? Why don't yer just *sod* off?'

Next day, I heard off Denise that Cathy'd gone out with Simon that night. He couldn't afford the pictures, so he took her round the Asda. They had a coffee in the café bit, and a scone each. And he put his little red blob on her mouth for a second, but nothing else.

You could tell, and all. The King was all quiet and serious next day, not mouthing off as normal. Never even give us a song at break. Cath was funny, too. Wouldn't talk to no one but Denise. We didn't like it at all.

Still, there was work to be done. The show was all set for four-thirty. We had to get some drums, and bouncers, and a place to meet up.

There ain't a lot of room in the first year cloakrooms. Even so, there was a good forty of us crammed in there after school. Carlo was going spare making sure everyone had got the routine straight.

'Remember,' he goes. 'No one makes a sound. Then the slow handclap. Then "Off! Off! Off!" Then the stones. Right? Mike'll give the signals.'

Mike O'Grady taps his chest.

'Let's move,' says Carlo.

The crowd start moving for the steps up to the door.

It's like some great caterpillar, all swaying and squashing. But before it gets very far, the door flies open. It's Spits Morris, and he looks desperate.

'It's off!' he goes. 'Split up, everyone! The show's off!'

Newt pushes his way through. 'Who says?' he yells back.

'They know! There's teachers all over the field! They stopped Andy with the bin lids!'

'Shit! Someone squealed!'

Carlo sets off through the crowd, pulling it all apart. It's Cathy he's after.

'You're the squealer, aintcha?' he goes, pushing Cath into the wall. 'Say you ain't!'

'Grow up, Carlo.'

'See! She never denied it! She squealed 'cos she's gone *soft* on little darling Slimy-Wimey! She couldn't bear to see 'im shown up for the *jerk* he is!'

Cath looks half-scared, and half-mad. Suddenly she stares up, over Carlo's shoulder. There, at the door, is the King himself.

Carlo wheels round. The King walks down the steps. The crowd shut up.

'An 'ere 'e is,' says Carlo. 'The *man* 'imself.'

'Leave 'er alone,' says Simon. 'She ain't 'urt you.'

The crowd splits apart. Carlo moves through.

'Who are you to tell me what to do, eh?'

The King stands with his legs apart. They're shaking. 'You know who I am,' he says.

'That's right,' says Carlo. He reaches Simon, and pokes him hard on the shoulder. 'A little dog.'

Carlo pokes again, and the King starts stumbling backwards. 'A little dog what thinks it's bleedin' *Elvis Presley*,' says Carlo. 'Go sniff someone else's bum, will yer?'

Simon's reached the wall. Suddenly, he grabs hold of Carlo's arm. 'Don't forget somefin,' he goes.

'Oh yeah?' goes Carlo. 'Wassat, then?'

'You're my bodyguard, Carlo.'

Carlo's face splits. 'You 'ear that?' he says to the crowd. 'I'm Fido's bodyguard!'

'*Leave him alone*!' yells Cathy. She's crying.

'Shut your face, traitor!' goes Carlo.

'Don't talk to her like that!' says the King.

'You in love wiv 'er?' goes Carlo. 'You in love wiv 'er, then?'

Simon snaps. He lashes out at Carlo, with this wild swing. Carlo ducks back, then grabs the King's weedy forehead with his hand. Simon's stick-arms windmill away in space. Shouts of 'Fight! Fight!' come up from the others. The King's out of his head, but he still can't hit a thing. Carlo's just teeing him up. Picking his time to flatten him.

Then Lanky Binney arrives.

'Break it up, the two of you!'

Binney pounces down three steps in one, spilling bodies all over the shop. Carlo breaks off. Straight off, Simon hits him. If Binney'd been a second slower, the King'd have been dead.

'I said *cut* it, you two! You're like a pair of animals! You should be behind bars being fed a banana!'

Carlo hangs his head, like a million times before. 'Yes, sir,' he mumbles.

'And you, Mr Waites! You've been leading up to this, haven't you?'

The King heaves for his breath. Slow and steady, his eyes come up.

'*Haven't* you, *Mr Waites*?'

Simon lifts his finger. Then his face twists itself into this real vicious mask.

'*Stick* it, Binney,' he says. 'Don't tell *me* what to do!'

It took six of us to hump him to Wilson's office.

Well, if Simon Waites wanted to make trouble for himself, that was his lookout. That's what everyone said. You've never seen a fan club melt away so fast. Once he'd been stood up in assembly, there wasn't a soul so much as knew his name.

I still can't believe it all happened, really. When I watch him now, copying off the board, petrified he'll miss a comma, I try and picture him back in Smokers' Corner. I just can't do it.

Still, what's he got to worry about? He'll get his O-levels all right now, some boring job, cash to buy a place to live and that. More than most of us will. He slaves away, we muck about, everything's back to normal. And everyone's sort of happy about it.

One thing, though. You can't get no sense out of some of these first years. 'When's 'e gonna stop pretendin'?' they keep saying. 'Don't be thick,' you have to tell them. '*This* ain't pretendin'. *This* is 'ow 'e really is. Him being the King, *that* was pretendin'.'

'Nah,' they say to you. ''E ain't really like that. 'E's just 'avin' you on.'

Threads

JANE GARDAM

●●●●

I got a great grandad going on ninety. He lives next
door to us with my gran (who's his daughter) because
she won't hear of Homes. Old folks going into them,
like. She says it's something we could take notice of from
the Japanese. They think it's the dregs, putting old folks
away. And that's remarkable from my gran because she
had a son in the war in Japanese hands and she never
saw him more.

We live in Grangetown. Four generations in one street.
It's not usual these days though not unheard of in
Grangetown.

My great grandad's no golden oldie, mind. My dad
says he's a dreadful old man. Keeps his daughter running
after him all day and half the night. 'Where's me pills!'
'Fetch me walking aid.' 'See to me foot.' 'Change me
bed.'

I never liked him. Not even when I was young. He
just sits scowling, moving his foot up and down on the
stirrup of the caliper. Squeaking. He makes this sort of
grunt all the time. My dad says he's the only person he's
ever met who snores when he's awake. He chews with
his mouth and there's nothing in it. He never takes notice
of me. Not ever. He never liked girls. He keeps on about

having no grandsons, nor great-grandsons. His teeth keep dropping.

Well, I got stuck with him this Saturday afternoon. I like my gran and she wanted to go down the Redcar library where you can get a coffee. My mam was busy and my dad working—not that he'd have grandad-sat if he hadn't been working. Not him. They said, 'Well, Karen can sit with him. For an hour. She's near fourteen. All she's to do is watch him for falls and run for his bottle if he needs it and empty it for him. It'll do her no harm.'

I carried on at them. Once I wouldn't. I was O.K. with people once. I'd have said all right once, nice as pie. I don't know what's come over me these days. I hate thirteen.

But I like my gran, like I said, and she hardly gets out. When the nurse comes to bath great grandad she'll do a dash down the post office for his pension. And for her pension. And maybe look in a couple of shop windows after the fashions. And that's all she gets. She's nearly seventy but she loves fashions. She likes her hair right, too, but it has to be shampoo and set only—there's no time for perms. She has to be thinking of him all the time—washing and ironing and cooking mushy food because of his gums. Collecting his pills from the surgery. Getting his lagers in. And not anything much in the way of thank-yous.

While she's out he'll walk up and down, up and down the passage on his walking frame and if he can he'll fall over to give her the frights when she comes running back in. My mam says, 'He's a tyrant. She'll go first. Remember I've said it. She'll go first.'

Well, this Saturday I didn't mind in the end sitting

there with great grandad because I'd got my period and I was feeling terrible. All I wanted was to sit still with a hot-water bottle and watch the football and not speak. When they'd gone, Mam and Gran, I humped myself down by the imitation coals on a stool, and folded my arms on my stomach and rocked myself about. He just sat there, in his special chair—it's like a throne—with his arms arranged over his walking frame and grunted away, paying me no attention.

They'd given him that telly gadget. A thing you hold in your hand and press. Well, you hardly have to press. You can just about breathe on the switch. When you do the television changes programme. It's like magic. Like an invisible thread. One minute you're seeing them tearing up and down all mud and curls and kissing each other and everyone going mad in the stadium above the advertisements for brandy; then you're in a kitchen with sunshine and copper pans and a mother all apple blossom and aprons like you never see, pouring cocoa into mugs for a male model and a couple of soppy kids in a garden like seed packets. Then whoops on the invisible thread and we're in black and white nostalgia valley and girls with patent leather lipstick and eyes like meat plates gazing at men in trilby hats and cigarettes at angles and someone's playing violins out of sight.

My great grandad was still over the moon at this present. Over the moon. He even sometimes stopped snoring. 'Ha,' he kept saying, 'saves the carpet.' 'Ha—what's this next trash then?' 'Ha—it's a goal. Looks as though the bugger's worth his transfer after all.' He'd only had the thing a week.

I didn't have to do anything. Not even answer him. Just sit there and at four o'clock get him his cup of tea.

So I sat and got warm over the electric bars and held on to my stomach and sucked a hanky end.

All of a sudden I noticed there was a silence and I opened my eyes. I'd fallen asleep with my head against the side of the mantelpiece and I'd jerked up. 'Are you all right then?' I asked. I see he's looking over at me. Munching.

'Aye, I'm all right,' he says. 'Are you all right? Who are you?'

'Well, I'm Karen.'

'Oh aye. I get you mixed. Are you Brian's?'

'Uncle Brian's dead,' says I, 'in Singapore. Long since.'

'Oh aye,' he says and sits and broods at the empty oblong of the telly.

I say, 'You switched it off.'

'Aye,' he says. 'There's not owt. Nowt that's anything.'

'Don't you want the football?'

'They're all rubbish. Not a player among them.'

'Did you play football once?'

'No. Never. Never played anything. Work—that's what I did.'

He munched his lips and squeaked his caliper.

'D'you want your tea?' asks I and he looks across at me and says, 'You looked twined.'

'Twined?'

'Aye. Are you taken poorly?'

'No. I'll get you a cup of tea. I've got a pain, that's all.'

'It'll be your time of the month,' he said and I just looked.

Honest—I just looked.

It was right disgusting. I thought, you right disgusting old man.

I'll tell you something. I'll talk to my mam about most

65

things—about drugs at school and sleeping with lads, and the pill, and whether people ought to live together before they're married like some I could mention in this family. (And it's not that I think it's wicked. Just disgusting and not romantic. It takes the poetry out and it's made our Marion a different person—all strong views and shouting. Brazen, if you want to know. And you should just see *him*!) Yes. I talk about a lot of things even to my dad and I talk to my gran about real things like death and why we are born and the stars and what started them, and religions.

But I won't talk about periods. No, I will not. Not even at school on games days. There's some can and some can't. You're born like it. Actually it has taken quite a bit of doing to write the word down. The whole thing's disgusting anyway. There was this girl in the church choir the only time I ever went. First question she asked. She was fourteen and I was ten. Disgusting.

And here's my great grandad near on ninety talking about it matter-of-fact like he was a doctor or something. Which he never was. He was a farmer's son and then a leather merchant in Clitheroe.

And he scarcely knows who I am minute to minute. Yet he can speak it outright.

'It's from the moon,' he says. 'Women is in the hands of the moon. Like the tides. The time of the month. We're all on threads of one sort and another. It's best to be in charge of them, that's the secret. Hold 'em tight or snip 'em through.' He breathed on the switch and the invisible thread tweaked the screen into life.

Well, before I *died*, I went out to the kitchen and boiled the kettle.

'Here's your tea then, great grandad,' I said. He

66

was gazing at the television but the screen had gone blank again and the switch he'd let fall to the floor. 'Put the cup down,' he says. 'Pull my table over. Look sharp now. Did you sugar it?' And he sat there slurping the tea through his loose teeth from the awful baby cup thing with the two handles.

'The moon,' he says next, 'I'll tell you something about the moon. And nowt to do with women and girls.'

Squeak, squeak, squeak went the shoe on the caliper stirrup until I could have squealed. I tried to joke a bit. 'Armour must have sounded like you,' I said, but he just chewed his cheeks. He's no sense of humour.

'The moon,' he says. 'Nineteen-eight. We had a lad living with us on our farm at home. Irish boy. Couldn't read nor write. Skin and bone. They used to come over to Cumberland looking for work. Stood about all over the North-West at the hirings.'

'Hirings?'

'Well, *hirings*. You—that's to say the farmers—would all go down the nearest market town a couple of times a year and walk about the square and there'd be little clusters of them—maybe a hundred. There'd be a wall and chalked up on it "For Hire". Not only Irish—Scotch fellers and Yorkshire and far afield. Lasses too. Standing about for hire and you'd take the strongest-looking.'

'What, people?' says I. 'Buying people?'

'No. Hiring. Aye. Nineteen-seven. Nineteen-eight. You'd take them home with you agreeing for a twelve-month or six months or just a haytime. The ones not chosen on account of being weak-looking stood around proud. They'd doss down in a hedgeback the night and then walk on to the next place.

'Well, there was this lad once—Michael—a poor thing,

and the boss, my father, was a kind man especially when he'd had a drink, which everyone had hiring days, and he more than the rest. He'd been that long in the Public this day, to tell truth, most of the strong lads had been snapped up before he ever saw them. I hung about waiting and at last Father comes rolling along with his wing collar under one ear and his green bowler hat on the back of his head— farmers dressed up them days for occasions. Here's this poor weak-headed little thing still standing there all alone with his mouth half open and his long Irish arms dangling out of his sleeves. "Come on then, lad," says the boss. "Six months at five pounds, paid at finish, and here's your luck penny." You had to give luck penny—which was a shilling—for right feelings, at hirings. That's all you did. No insurance. Nothing written. You learned them plenty, mind. It was being apprenticed. Six months and his keep. Their box would come on after on the train and they never had money for it. We'd pay the guard—meet it up at the nearest station after maybe a week and fetch it home on the cart.

'Well, this lad Michael was eighteen and I was eleven and he was like a brother to me. Work! He could work. Never to be called twice of a winter's morning. Five o'clock up for the cows and half of them milked before the boss even got to the byre. A fair demon he was for stooking the corn. He could fork a stack faster and straighter than the best—once he'd put weight on with a bit of proper cooking. You should have seen him eat. Plate a foot high. And he'd go down into it rather than take the food up into him. He didn't drink. Which was a queer carry on for an Irishman. He said his mam had never let him. One thing he could do was shoot. He had this old gun. It'd been his father's. It was about all he

68

owned. He and I'd be away off shooting many a summer night over the rough ground. Rooks for a pie. Cushets. Duck. He had a straight eye.

'Never a straight head though. There was a weakness there. He wasn't a thinker in any way. And not much will to him. "Simple," my mother used to say. "Poor Michael. He's a floddum. Well nigh a halfwit." My father says, "Nay. He'll do. There's nowt amiss with Michael except when the moon's full. He's not got what it takes to stand up against the moon," and we'd all laugh. There's supposed to be something funny about folks going daft at time of full moon. Though it never seemed that funny to me. Even before Michael.

'When the moon was full, see, Michael wouldn't work. He couldn't work. It seemed as if he just couldn't. He'd lie up in the barn and never rise off his bed. Now it sounds a terrible thing that he had to sleep in the barn but it weren't out of common. There was two—three cubicles up there with a bed and a chair and a box in each and a hook for clothes. We'd had three men once but times was harder now and we couldn't afford but one. He'd come down and wash at the yard pump, and his needs he'd do behind the hedges. He ate his food with us—across at another table in the kitchen, but in the same room. We weren't savages. We'd try teaching him whist and nap of an evening too, but he couldn't get his mind round the numbers on the cards.

'When the moon was full though, Michael was no-where in the kitchen. He never came in for his food and he never came down to the pump to wash. Nor put on his clothes. No more did he go off after the cows for milking, nor pick up the chain to take the bull to the water, nor down to the stack-yard, nor away shooting cushets with me. The gun stood propped against the wall of his barn stall, and the boss would roar and create, but Michael would just lie there with his eyes wide open, not speaking, humped on his iron bed under his blanket and old raggedy coat, watching the ivy at the barn slats flickering. "Leave him be," the boss'd say at finish. "It's the moon. He's one of them poor devils affected. He's beyond us all. Three days and he'll be back."

'My mother would take food up there to Michael against the boss's orders but he never touched it. She'd set it on the chair beside him, talking kind and natural.

'Then a day or so after, he'd be down at the pump again, smiling round, washing himself and the plates Mother had brought. Whistling. He'd cleared the plates all at once with his fingers to such a polish they scarcely needed water.

'Well, he left.

'We had to put him off after next harvest. Times was bad. I walked with him to the lonning gate and said goodbye and he went off to the next hiring. He had a better coat than when he came for we'd given him the boss's old one. There was a good shirt in his bundle and some butter and a bit of bacon and five shillings over his five pounds. He looked a better buy than six months previous, his gun across his shoulder almost jaunty. He loved that gun.

'Well next thing we know he's up for murder.

'Michael up for murder. "The gentlest lad we ever had," my father says. "Never a drink in him. Never a word of bad language."

'It seems the next farmer to hire him had been a brute however. Yelled at him and cussed at him morning to night and put him out of the house after supper like a dog. When Michael came to his funny turn at the time of the full moon he'd pulled him from his bed and kicked him. The second day he did it again and Michael upped from the floor—quiet, sweet-charactered Michael—and took the gun and shot the farmer through the head.

'My father, the boss, put on his wing collar and his bowler hat and his button boots and his best suit and went to speak for Michael at the trial. Miles away. Over in the North East. Further than my father had ever been in his life. But it did no good. He told them about the full moon. But it did not a bit of good. They hanged Michael. In Durham gaol. Nineteen-eight. He was just nineteen.'

'Now then!' In comes my gran all pink in the face in what looks very like a new scarf, and carrying parcels and two library books and followed by my mam with the supermarket shopping and a big potted plant.

'Are you right then?' says Mam. 'How's he been? You saw to his tea? My, I could do with some. Mother's brought you a plant, Grandad—begonia, the kind you like. Only a pound. Whatever's the matter with the telly? It's not on.'

'Are you better?' asks my gran. 'Sit still and I'll get the tea.'

'I'm fine,' says I. 'Great. I'll get it. I'll get it for all of us. There's nothing wrong with me at all.'

'That's a good lass,' says Gran, and follows me to the kitchen. 'Has he been difficult? He's looking very wambly. It'd be dull for you—all alone on a Saturday afternoon. Your poor grandad, there's not much there any more I'm afraid. We'll all come to it. He's got interest and memory for nothing now, poor soul.'

Mackerel

EMMA SMITH

●●●●

When Alastair McIntyre was five years old his mother disappeared out of his life. Alastair remembered her being there, and then her not being there. She went off with someone. His father, an electrician who worked for the Council, never referred to the man his mother went off with, nor to the circumstances of her going off, nor indeed ever again, except when it was unavoidable, to Alastair's mother.

Alastair had a far clearer recollection of his father's refusal to let him be taken away by the authorities than he had of his mother's mistily sudden departure. The precise words that were spoken above his head he forgot, but the fierce tone of his father's voice and the feel of his father's hands gripping his shoulders in the presence of strangers he remembered.

'I can raise the boy myself,' Douglas McIntyre had declared on that occasion, very forcibly, again and again. 'Nobody's going to put my son in a home while I'm here to stop it. I'm his father. I can manage.'

Impressed by such resolve, and in view of the fact that Mr McIntyre was a respectable tradesman with a steady job, and of the further ascertained facts that he was not a drinker, not a philanderer, paid his rent on the nail, eschewed hire-purchase, and that, moreover, his neigh-bours were willing to help out—in view of all this information, the social services finally decided he should be allowed to have a shot, anyway, at managing.

And for the next four and a half years Douglas McIntyre did somehow contrive to give the boy what was officially considered to be an adequate upbringing.

Then, one dark and icy December morning, a milk lorry skidded into a bus queue, and Alastair's father vanished from sight and sound as utterly and with as little warning as his mother had done before.

There being now no one to stop it, and no alternative, Alastair, who had reached the age of nearly ten, was put in a home. Or rather, he was put in a series of short-stay homes that culminated, when a vacancy cropped up at last, in a long-stay establishment. Long-stay, short-stay, they were all the same to Alastair—indistinguishable: merely places in which to pass the time while waiting.

He was waiting for his father; and this in spite of having attended his father's funeral. Still he expected to hear, sooner or later, the knock at the door, the ring at the bell, that would mean his father had come to fetch him away. The expectation lay buried so deep in his heart, and in the furthest recesses of his mind, that he was unaware of what sustained him.

Waiting was more than merely a habit. Those hundreds of afternoons when he sat patiently, mostly silent, in the various kitchens of the various obliging neighbours had always ended with the desired result, until it had grown to seem infallible as a law of nature: waiting produced his father.

As to the kindly women whose kitchens he once occu-pied, their efforts to make a pet of Alastair had been unavailing. Try as they might, he would attach himself to none of them. His attention was fixed elsewhere.

'Why don't you let me boil you an egg, Alastair love? It's a terrible long time for a child your age to have to wait for his tea.'

'No thank you, Mrs Campbell—Mrs Carter—Mrs Hitchens,' he would reply; his father had taught him to be polite. 'My dad'll be back soon.'

His dad had always been back, without fail, for their tea together; had never been late. A vague uneasy subliminal sense that something must be keeping him now, something not his dad's fault, haunted the son of the man who was dead.

During the years that followed the funeral, the meanwhile years as it were, Alastair McIntyre strove to behave according to his father's instructions on what he ought and what he ought not to do, and also, which was a good deal harder, to guide himself by his father's opinions; or by as much of them as memory could salvage. Such tangible assets as football and bike having been mislaid somewhere along the way, these instructions and opinions were all, in the end, that his father had left him; all he had left of his father. They constituted his essential survival kit.

He used to lie awake in the darkness of strange beds, anxiously checking over and over the bits and pieces of his invisible inheritance, trying to codify them for greater convenience: *Brush your teeth, brush your hair, brush your shoes on the mat, wash your hands before you eat, tell the truth, shut the door, go to school*—

'You have to go to school, Alastair.'

He heard his father's voice, clear as a bell.

'You have to be educated—everyone does. I tell you

this—and don't you ever forget it!—education is the answer. They canna beat us, Alastair! Show them what you're worth, boy!'

His heart in the darkness thudded faster. Who were They? And what exactly was it that he had never to forget? *Brush your teeth, brush your hair—*

'There's aye a logic—aye an answer! Come on, Alastair—use your brains, lad! Stick to it! Never say die! Think, boy!—think!'

The familiar phrases, exhortations, rang aloud inside his head, confused and confusingly. He heard his father; saw him in snapshot glimpses, mending the radio, shaving, punting the Christmas football clean across an enormous rainy space: heard him, saw him, in a jumble of pictures and echoing captions that, as the months and then the years went by, fuzzed and faded, until little by little survival came to depend for Alastair McIntyre on a single word: *education*; its four syllables magically summarizing everything his missing father stood for. Education was the hand that would lead him out of the wilderness.

By the time he was fifteen Alastair held an unbroken record for school attendance; and this in a neighbourhood where truancy was rampant. He never complained of stomach-ache. He never allowed any illness, invented or real, to keep him from going to school. He went every day the school doors were open, and he stayed all day until they closed. He was uniquely immune, it appeared —at any rate amongst the seventeen boys and girls of St George's Residential Home—to all forms of the epidemic disease of absenteeism.

In other ways as well he was exceptional. He neither drank, nor smoked, nor swore; although, being a singularly silent boy, this last eccentricity was hardly noticeable. Nor had he acquired the usual supplementary benefit of a probation officer, never having smashed so much as a window, or nicked so much as a bag of sweets in his life.

These abstentions were not due to religious fervour, as might have been supposed, his politely disinterested attitude towards God resembling what had formerly been his attitude towards the helpful neighbours. The Almighty, he once observed cryptically and reverting to the long discarded accent of his earlier childhood, in his opinion 'didna have the answer'. It sounded as if he were quoting.

Judged by the standards of his peers, Alastair—religion apart—was extraordinary, and marked out as a consequence for persecution. But he was not persecuted. Perhaps it was his local fame on the football field that saved him; or perhaps it was his talent for climbing. His powers as a climber were legendary in the district: he would shin without hesitation up any tree, any wall or drainpipe; had been known to balance, unsmiling, three storeys high, along the centre ridge of the Home's roof to disentangle a kite from a chimney-pot. Or perhaps what preserved him was that he could be relied on, although law-abiding himself, to tell no tales. Whatever the reason, or reasons, Alastair McIntyre was spared the mockery of his fellows.

At St George's, indeed, they were rather proud of their freak; a little wary of him, too. Something about the normally pacific Alastair, a certain fierceness fiercely controlled, the occasional eruption of an inner volcanic fire, warned them off provoking his rage. If hands were ever imprudently laid on him, he could fight, and did so, like a boy possessed by a demon.

Mackerel, they called him. And Mackerel was a funny bugger, said Errol and Barry and Bruce and Marilyn and Steve. But they said it with a sort of an affection. To which affection Alastair responded not at all. He was not unfriendly; not sullen, or sulky, in the least. He was always perfectly civil. But his attention continued to be focused elsewhere. In the social services file on Alastair McIntyre he was described as *withdrawn. Aloof* would have been a better word.

During the summer of his sixteenth year Alastair and the rest of the gang at St George's were taken on a week's camping holiday to the Pembrokeshire coast. Until then their only experience of the seaside had been the Home's annual day-trip to Clacton, or sometimes, for the sake of a change of candyfloss and one-armed bandits, to Southend.

This Welsh adventure was the inspiration of a controversial young man, Philip Halliwell, who taught English at Alastair's school, and who had recently, with his wife Linda, moved into the street adjacent to St George's Residential Home. In a state of angry enthusiasm he had swept aside every objection, over-ridden every obstacle, borrowed camping gear and a battered old minibus from a nearby collapsing Youth Club, squeezed from a reluctant Municipal Council the modest amount of funding required, and driven his load of grinning faces triumphantly off to confront them with what he said was *real* sea—the mighty crested rollers of the Atlantic Ocean.

It had been an entire success, the TV-less candyfloss-less holiday. St George's junior residents had all returned from Wales as bouncingly healthy and as boastfully pleased with themselves as though returning to civilization from the conquered peaks of Kinchinjunga; all except for Alastair. On him the Atlantic Ocean had had a different effect.

He had felt an affinity with it at once. The unceasing voices of wind and waves had seemed to him to be speaking a dialect that was very ancient and very mysterious, and full of a wisdom he could almost understand. Afterwards he was quieter, if that were possible, than before. In July of the following year, having completed his State-sponsored education, he left school.

Philip Halliwell, the English teacher, left the same school as Alastair the same day and also for ever. He had been offered a Research Fellowship at a New Zealand university on the strength of his book, *It's a Waste of Time, Sir*. The offer came as a distinct relief to the outraged members of the School Board, who had decided to get rid of him in any case, but who preferred their unsatisfactory teachers to agree to the more dignified course of resigning.

Dignity was hardly to be expected, however, of Philip Halliwell, a most uncomfortable person to have on the staff, and doubly so now that his upsetting views regarding the educational system had got into print and undeniably made a splash. The School Board had intended, before being let off the hook by New Zealand, to dismiss him on the justifiable grounds of his unorthodox teaching methods; or non-teaching methods, according to some.

'His classes are Bedlam,' said the Headmaster.

They were certainly noisy; a noise to which Alastair McIntyre had not contributed. He used to sit, that final year, at the back of Mr Halliwell's crowded classes—the only classes in the whole school which always were crowded—impervious to the surrounding hubbub, hearing it as no more than a dim outside echo of the clamour of gulls and the thunderous crash of waves that he was listening to inside his head.

On the evening of the day Alastair left school he called in at Philip Halliwell's house to ask him where the camping equipment had been borrowed from the year before, so that he might apply to the same source himself. He was going back to Wales on his own. His plan was to hitch-hike. He had cash enough, saved up from his pocket-money to buy food with once he arrived. All he needed was a tent and a sleeping-bag.

Mrs Halliwell, a pretty fair-haired girl wearing jeans and sandals, opened the door to him. She was holding her baby, Susie, eight months old. Pregnancy had prevented her joining the St George's expedition last summer. A little brown rough-haired mongrel terrier pushed by her legs to sniff at the visitor's ankles.

'Oh, hello, Alastair.' They already had a doorstep acquaintance. He could see a clutter of boxes and baggage in the passage behind her. 'Phil's out, I'm afraid, but he won't be long.'

She took him into the kitchen and handed him a cup of tea and was very chatty and frank. They were off to Pembrokeshire themselves the following day, as a matter of fact, for a couple of weeks. Phil had to make up his mind about this job in New Zealand, yes or no, definitely. He had accepted the Fellowship, but he had still not actually signed the contract. It was a big decision—to go and live on the other side of the world. Because if they did go, they would go for keeps: they would emigrate.

'Everyone says it's a marvellous country, New

Zealand—and of course it's a marvellous job. We're terribly lucky—' But she sounded oddly dubious.

Alastair was welcome, she told him, to borrow the little tent and the cooking-stove that Phil had used as a student, years ago. And they had a spare sleeping-bag, too. Probably they could even manage to squash him into a corner of their antiquated van, if he could put up with having Trotty dumped on top of him. Did he like dogs? What a pity he should be setting off alone, though, for his holiday—not half as much fun! She presumed that Mr Bolton had given permission—had he? Mr Bolton was the amiable but, in Philip Halliwell's view, the deplorably unenterprising father-in-charge of St George's Residential Home.

'He's not bothered,' said Alastair, shrugging.

Philip returned, and matters were duly arranged. But later, on reflection, Linda began to query the justice of what she had so spontaneously promoted. There were sixteen other boys and girls at St George's.

'It doesn't seem fair for us to be taking only one of them—'

'Fair!' cried Philip, boiling over in a flash. His mood was nowadays unpredictably volatile. 'Fair! Is there anything fair about those kids' lives? I ask you, Lin! Where do you suppose they'll be in a few weeks from now—all of them? On the dole queue! And not just the St George's bunch, either.' Unemployment in the area was high, and rising steadily. 'That's what we educate our kids for today. Educate them!' He pushed his plate away, as though the sight of a baked potato sickened him. 'Old Wetherspoon was perfectly right when he called my classes Bedlam. So they were. I didn't teach those kids a thing. What, in Heaven's name, was I to teach them?

How not to care that they've been born unwanted?—
born with *redundant*, Lin—that word—that criminal
word—stamped on their foreheads like the mark of
Cain?'

'Oh, Phil—' She pressed her own wanted unredundant
baby closer to her breast.

'I'm glad it's over—over for me, at least. I can't stand
it any more, Lin. Thank God for New Zealand!'

He spoke as though their future had been settled. But
then in the next breath he spoke as though it had not
been settled.

'I thought the whole point of us belting off to
Pembrokeshire was so as to have the chance of making
our minds up in peace. Fat lot of peace there'll be
with that young Mackerel hung round our necks,' he
grumbled.

But Alastair McIntyre had never hung himself around
the neck of anyone. When they arrived the following
evening at their destination, a steeply sloping field over-
looking the Bay of Porth Mawr, Alastair crawled from
the van, stiff-legged with cramp, thanked the Halliwells
as politely as though they had been total strangers to
him, grabbed hold of his bundles, and promptly made
off uphill. Rather disconcerted, they watched him go.
Trotty, his travelling companion, whined, and then
barked, and then trotted after him. They called her back.

'What a funny boy,' said Linda. 'And his eyes, Phil—
have you noticed?—they're funny—something about
them. Do you think he takes drugs?'

'*Him*?—take drugs? Good Heavens, no!—not Alastair.'

He pitched his tent at the very top of the field, as far
from the Halliwells' tent as it was possible to be. Since

he thus unmistakably signified his wish to be left alone, they left him alone—except, that is, for Trotty—and were thankful to do so. They had their own problem to deal with.

Philip hired a deep-sea rod and went fishing off the rocks of one of the headlands—fishing, in his experience, being the best method for coming to grips with any problem. Linda spent the day on the beach with Susie and a restless Trotty and several scores of other families and their dogs. Alastair spent it climbing cliffs.

He climbed the cliffs up and down and sideways. He wandered miles along the cliff-path and over the gorse- and heather-covered headlands. He watched, unseen, Philip Halliwell fishing, and Linda playing with her baby. He said nothing to anyone, not even when he bought a pork pie and a bottle of lemonade in the shop in the car-park for his dinner, and a packet of fish-and-chips off the mobile canteen for his tea.

He was done with people. The voices he heard were the voices he had been hearing for the last year: those age-old indifferent voices of water surging and sucking in and out of caves; the voices of sea-birds wheeling, drifting on the wind; and the voice of the wind, the confidential tireless wordless voice of the wind in his ears, whispering, fluttering, as it endlessly fluttered and whispered in the dry grasses at his feet. Voices, all, that asserted nothing, denied nothing, promised nothing.

At the end of the day he sat in front of his tiny borrowed orange tent and watched the sun sink in a clear sky towards the sea's horizon. Soon it would be dark, and then above him for company there would be a million stars, and for further company, should he have need of it, the beam of the lighthouse that swept across the bay as regular as clockwork on the count of eight. Already the lighthouse had started to wink in preparation: one, two, three, four, five, six, seven, *wink;* one, two—

'Alastair!'

Linda Halliwell, in shorts and a yellow sweater, and carrying her baby, was ascending the field. The little dog, Trotty, rushed on ahead of them to greet him ecstatically. He scrambled up, confused.

'I've brought you your supper.' She was dangling a fish. 'Mackerel for Mackerel,' she laughed; but hastening, when she saw that he flinched at the nickname, to repair her mistake: 'What a smashing view you have up here, Alastair—much better than ours is. You're so high! It's windier, though—a lot. Here—catch hold of Susie a sec.'

He held the baby, carefully, while she tied back her hair with a scarf. And then Linda, retrieving Susie from him, stood beside Alastair and looked at his view for several minutes without speaking, silenced by his silence.

She went down the darkening field, past the other campers' tents, beginning now to glow like green and orange paper lanterns, to their tent at the bottom, and she said to her husband:

'He worries me, that boy—he really does.'

'All our kids today worry me,' Philip answered her, very brusque.

'Yes, but he's got a secret, Phil—something awful. I'm sure he has. And we'll never know what it is, because he can't say.'

But the next morning, to her surprise, he sought her out on the beach where she sat with Susie and Trotty. She concealed her surprise. Philip was away on the rocks again somewhere, fishing.

At the mention of Philip's name: 'They sacked him—didn't they,' said Alastair, abruptly; a statement, not a question. He brushed off her reference to New Zealand. 'They was going to sack him anyway—*wasn't* they? On account of us lot—all that talking and shouting and that.'

'Well, yes—I daresay they were,' she admitted.

'So is that what it is then—education?' Alastair persisted; '—what *he* says it is—just letting kids talk?'

'No—of course not. But talking's a start—or it can be. It depends on—well, on everything else—the circumstances.'

He was making, she realized, a supreme effort, this uncommunicative boy, to communicate with her. And she therefore tried herself in return to explain to him, here on the swarming holiday beach, her husband's philosophy of communication; his dedicated commitment to the power and the beauty of language; his belief that it should be written, spoken, used, and understood, and enjoyed, by everyone. 'You ought to read his book,' she finished, with a dismaying sense of her eloquence making no impression on Alastair. He lay at full length, unanswering, his face averted. 'I'll lend you a copy, if you like, when we get home.'

'No thanks,' he said, drawing circles in the sand.

'But it's good, Alastair—honestly.' She was rather affronted.

'Not for me, it's not. I can't read.'

He stunned her. And then, recovering: 'Oh, Alastair,' she cried, impulsively, 'I'll teach you to read.'

'Will you? When?' He looked up at her with derision over his hunched and protective shoulder. 'You're going to New Zealand.'

84

She imagined that Alastair McIntyre had divulged his awful secret, and it seemed to her, in consideration of the effect it had on Philip, to be awful indeed. Philip was aghast at the news. That a pupil of his—'one of my kids'—could attend his English classes for two years and yet be illiterate, and he not know it until this moment, struck him as the epitome of his own failure. But he presently discovered what was far worse.

That afternoon, while fishing off the rocks, and too much troubled in his thoughts to be having much success with this occupation either, he glanced up and saw Alastair perched above, watching him; or perhaps merely gazing out to sea. He was afraid that when he waved and cupped his hands to yell an invitation, the boy would simply vanish, but instead Alastair McIntyre climbed expertly down, and was given a lesson in casting.

Again and again the long strong line whistled out across the slowly heaving huge Atlantic swells. Alastair, remarkably, got the knack of it almost at once, and the fish were suddenly plentiful, and every silver mackerel that came twisting up from the deep green fathoms of water was like the solution to a problem; so that a curious urge arose in Philip Halliwell to ask this boy for his advice. He wanted to shout at him above the noise of wind and breaking waves: *What shall I do?* It was Alastair, though, who shouted at Philip:

'I'm not going back!'

His face, freckled and burned a bright red by the sun, wore an exalted expression. Philip understood immediately what he meant, and how absolutely he meant it.

But Linda had to have the meaning explained to her. And when it was: 'Oh no, Phil!' she cried, and kept on crying, sick with horror, distraught. 'He can't! He mustn't! We've got to stop him—'

Phil warned her that the boy, Alastair, had made up his mind. He had decided.

She burst into tears afresh. 'To drown himself?—' she wailed.

'Yes. And Linda—stopping him won't be easy.'

Alastair's decision was not a spur of the moment affair. He had been contemplating it seriously ever since the previous July. He had now left school. The likelihood of his getting a job was remote. He had no family. Very soon he would have no home, the St George's children being required, upon reaching the age of eighteen, to remove themselves to some other address. Through thick and thin, year after year, he had clung on and on, waiting. What had the waiting been for? Alastair McIntyre recently concluded that he was the subject of a prolonged hoax: it had all been for nothing. Nothing!

He came in the same category as certain goods that he had heard Mr Bolton, when checking the store-room at St George's, describe as being "surplus to need". In which case it was stupid for him to stay. He might as well go. And if going, then what more suitable departure platform than here?—here, where the land that people lived on ended in tall cliffs, and the mighty ocean, quencher of flames and breath, began. He had worked it all out in his head. He had found, by himself and for himself, the logical answer.

This was Philip's version of some of the halting blurted fragments he had, with difficulty, extracted from Alastair as they sat on the rocks, and climbed the headland, and walked back to the tents together along the cliff path.

Linda's first instinct was to take Susie and run up the

field as fast as she could, and place her baby tenderly in Alastair's arms. Who, not made of ice, could resist the speechless appeal of her happy child? But Philip counselled against it. Rather than bringing about a miracle conversion, he said, she would be far more likely to scare Alastair off. And his wife, with sorrowful amazement, agreed:

'It's true—he doesn't even *see* Susie. The way he holds her, she could just as well be a parcel.'

Alastair would have to be won—if won at all—by reason, said Philip. Although he could neither read nor write, he was a blocked intellectual and a buried poet, and in that order; which was why argument and not emotion would be the more liable to prevail.

When Linda, startled, queried these titles of poet and intellectual, Philip replied impatiently: 'I mean that he has his faculties, Lin—his senses—in full measure, locked inside him. D'you want to know why he doesn't see our Susie? Because for two years he sat at the back of my classes and I didn't see him.'

'Oh Phil—no—that's not true.' She was shocked by the bitterness of his self-reproach.

'True enough. Well, now I've got nine days, Linda— nine days to convince that kid of mine by argument that he has to choose—as we all have to choose—to live and not to die: life, not death! And if I don't succeed—if he's not *convinced*, Lin—then whether sooner or whether later, one day he's going to say: No thanks!'

And Philip added, as clue to a comprehension of what made Alastair tick: 'My guess is, he's like his dad—the Scottish electrician.'

It was Linda then who startled her husband by saying, as she blew her nose: 'He's like you, Phil.'

'*Me?*' He was astonished. 'We're completely different.'

She, however, insisted that there was a similarity.

Philip Halliwell planned his campaign on the premise that this Mackerel was a mis-named fish who would have to be hooked with skill and afterwards played with subtlety and perseverance, otherwise he could very well break off the line and still be lost. He must be let alone, and not chased after. He must feel free to approach or retreat at will. It was Philip's job simply to be accessible, to stay put and be ready to make the most of whatever opportunity presented itself.

Such a strategy wore hard on the nerves of the strategists, and especially hard on Linda's nerves, she being the one least actively involved. Only when Alastair was in sight, when she could observe him for herself, sitting outside his tent or fetching water from the tap in the lane, only then was she able to breathe easily.

But mostly he was not in sight. All day he roamed abroad—who knew where?—wandering the beaches, the cliff-paths, the headlands. And sometimes it was not until after dark, when his orange tent bloomed at the top of the field like a tulip, that she knew he was home again, safe.

Philip tried to relieve his wife's painful unremitting anxiety. Alastair would remain safe, he assured her, anyway for as long as they were camping there themselves. The boy's politeness was the guarantee of that: he would never dream of disrupting the Halliwells' holiday so crudely. It would certainly be his intention to do what he was intending to do after they were gone.

'Then we mustn't ever go,' she cried, wildly. 'Never! Or Phil—we must make him come with us—*force* him to—'

'That's not what would solve it, Lin.'

'I know it's not,' she said.

All day he roamed—and who knew where? Trotty knew where. Trotty had adopted Alastair. From dawn to dusk, or later, she trotted gladly at his heels, returning to the Halliwells' tent at the bottom of the field, hungry, thirsty, tired and contented, when Alastair returned to his at the top. Each night she slept in her own basket. Linda groaned that the chance of persuasion available to so constant a companion should be wasted on Trotty, who was unequipped with an advocate's tongue. But Philip said:

'My darling Linda, if Trotty wasn't a dumb animal he'd never take her with him.'

Every morning directly after breakfast Philip set off with his rod and tackle for one of the less frequented headlands. In addition to the rod, his Mackerel bait consisted of buns and enough sandwiches for two and a large thermos of tea. He never knew when Alastair was going to turn up but some time during the day, unfailingly, boy and dog would materialize. Then, as though fulfilling the terms of a bargain tacitly agreed upon, the rod would be handed over, and Philip would watch while Alastair planted his legs wide for purchase and cast the long line far out across the green water, and reeled it in, and cast again and again, his eyes tranced. And it might be that he pulled out a fish, and it might be not.

They drank tea and they shared the sandwiches. And Philip, by dint of questioning, for nothing was volunteered, learned more, although not much more, about the Scottish electrician who had been knocked down by a lorry when Alastair was nine; piecing together from

89

the semi-obliterated scraps of childhood's memory the picture of an upright man, an independent man, a man who had urged his son to think for himself; a man who, above all else, had believed in education.

'He was always on at me, my dad, about *education*—schooling. How it was—you know—important, and that. He used to say it was the answer—education.'

'Well, and he was right.'

'You reckon?—I don't. I reckon as my dad was wrong,' said Alastair flatly, getting up and walking away.

But the next day he was back. He asked Philip: 'So what do you say it is, then?'

'Say what is?'

'Education. I mean—I don't know—what is it?'

Philip tried to be brief in his preliminary summarizing of the historical perspective; to condense his personal view of society, as it was and as it ought to be. Education itself he defined epigrammatically as that which enabled a human being, armed with the fullest possible knowledge and understanding, to declare: I shouldn't, and therefore I shan't; I can, and therefore I will. But of course education was much more than this. He talked and talked.

Alastair, silent again, sat munching sandwiches and gazing seawards. He may have been listening; or, equally, his ears may have been closed against his ex-teacher's impassioned monologue. After the boy had left him, Philip wondered, exhausted, if he had absorbed a single syllable. What had he been thinking about? Was it fishing? Or was it something else?

As the days went by Philip Halliwell grew increasingly desperate. Alastair's silence defeated him. It was a wall he could not breach, until at last, abandoning all subtleties of argument, he threw caution aside and harangued him openly.

'It's no good expecting answers to drop out of the sky, like—like manna from heaven—they won't. You have to search for them—struggle for them—die struggling, perhaps—people do! But to kill yourself—throw yourself away—*that's* not an answer to anything.'

And finally the volcano erupted. Eyes ablaze, half-choked, Alastair turned on him, stammering: 'Words! —words!—just *words*!'

'Yes—words!'

They stood as enemies, face to face on the rocks, a yard apart and both in a rage.

'Words are necessary,' Philip shouted. 'Words are marvellous! How in hell do you suppose we're any of us ever going to be able to understand each other properly—express ourselves properly—if we don't use words? How in hell can we pass on ideas—how can they survive—as they *do* survive, ideas, for longer than us, for centuries—if we don't have a language? People need ideas—ideas are food. Without ideas, people starve. Your father knew that—'

'My father's dead.'

'He didn't choose to be, poor chap. Your father was a practical man. He'd have told you, if he was here now, that to be dead is to be useless—wasted, Alastair! Life makes you *valuable*—because when you're alive you can think and feel, and ask questions, and search for those answers—answers for everyone, not for just yourself. People affect each other—don't you realize that? Everything we do, or say, has its effect on other human beings. What sort of a message will you be passing on if you quit? "I'm clearing out because things got too hard for me"?—'

He broke off sharply, conscious of Alastair's ironical—was it contemptuous?—unwavering stare. To whom—of whom—was he speaking?

Three nights before they were due to leave there was a storm. Linda lay awake, holding Susie close, and hearkening to the huge violence of wind and rain and waves in the world outside their frail shelter, thinking with a sick heart of fishermen and sailors who battled for their lives in drowning seas and of the boy, Alastair, who wanted only that the sea should swallow him.

By early morning the tempest was over. Rain still fell, but the wind had abated and the sky was clearing.

'Where's Trotty?'

Her basket had not been slept in.

'She must have stopped up with Alastair for the night, I suppose—no wonder!'

But when they went to fetch her back, Trotty was not there; and neither was Alastair. In the semi-darkness of dawn the interior of the little orange tent, with its neatly rolled sleeping-bag, had an ominously undisturbed appearance, as if he too had been absent all night. They looked at each other, horror-struck.

'Oh Phil—he hasn't—he wouldn't—'

But perhaps he would, and perhaps he had. A storm could have seemed a chance that was after all too good to miss, a heaven-sent alibi for disappearance. Oh, but surely—surely, said Linda, frantic for any straw to clutch, he would not at least have taken Trotty with him? And then, recalling his unfathomable eyes: he might have done, she thought—he could have done.

'Alastair?—never! No—no, Lin,' said Philip, at last, with the long sigh of a man waking from nightmare into the reality of a nightmarish world: 'If anything's happened to that kid, it was an accident—I'll swear to it. He won't have done it on purpose.'

'But he meant to,' she wept. 'He was going to kill himself—he wanted to die.' The tears poured down her cheeks.

'Yes—but Linda—he changed his mind. I know—I swear—he changed his mind.'

'*How* do you know?—how can you be so sure?'

'Because he despised me, Lin—that's why. He despised me for getting out. I saw it in his face. And that kid—that—that funny kid,' said Philip slowly, 'wouldn't ever do something he despised someone else for doing—believe me. I know it.'

They discovered Alastair almost at once, with Trotty, on a cliff-edge that was out of reach of the sea but scarcely broader than the width of a window-sill; both fully alive.

'She's broke a leg,' Alastair yelled up at them, 'and maybe more—ribs, maybe.'

Eventually, with the aid of ropes and lines and a shopping-bag, and various other ingenious devices; with the interested participation of a gathering number of campers aroused early by the emergency; with great care, and some daring—poor Trotty was rescued. Alastair, natural-born climber that he was, rescued himself.

'Silly little dog,' he burst out, the moment he had been helped and hauled over the edge and stood on the grass, wringing wet and shuddering uncontrollably from head to foot. 'She was chasing a rabbit, and she just went on—clean over the top. I thought she'd had her chips— RIP, and serve her right for being so daft—but she'll live to fight another day, I reckon—won't you, Trotty?'

She had gone over the cliff, and Alastair, guided by her piteous barks and whimpers, and groping for each toe- and finger-hold in the deepening dusk, had climbed his way down to her. By the time he arrived at Trotty's providential staging-post it was too dark to see more than the glimmer of surf beneath him; too dark, without risking disaster, to budge a further inch in any direction.

Midnight had brought them the storm. He described in graphic detail the fury of the elements: for he was dumb no longer. In a few hours he had grown to be, not merely voluble, but unstoppably garrulous. Whatever conversation may have passed between Alastair McIntyre and the savage and senseless waves below as they dashed themselves to pieces on unseen rocks during those hellish interminable hours of human solitude, it had transformed him, irreversibly. And in spite of his chattering teeth and the purple frozen flesh there was yet about him a curiously jubilant air, a sort of excited confidence.

'I knew you'd come for me, soon as it was light,' he said to Philip when they were trooping back towards the promised immediate paradise of bacon and eggs and sausages and hot tea.

Dawn had merged into day. The sun had risen and the sky was unclouded; but the breeze was fresh. He wore Philip's jersey, somebody else's anorak.

'Staying awake was the worst part of it. I knew, though, if I could only just manage to stick it out—hang on—somehow—till morning, you'd find me all right.'

And then Alastair gave utterance to a phrase which, coming as it did from this formerly speechless boy, his ex-pupil, so seared the imagination of the English-language-obsessed Philip Halliwell that any lingering doubts he might have had about his future course of action were resolved for him on the spot; also irreversibly.

'I knew,' said Alastair McIntyre, with a grin, 'as you wasn't a bloke who'd leave me to perish alone in the waters of darkness—would you, Phil? Hey, Linda—hand us over that girl of yours,' he called. 'I got something I want to say to her.'

Greatly wondering, Linda placed her precious baby in his still shivering arms. He held Susie as carefully as before, but not now as if she were a parcel.

'You got a nerve, you have—let go my nose! I reckon it's time you begun to express yourself properly, Susan Halliwell—and you can start with my name. It's easy—Mackerel! Go on, Susie—say it!' She shrieked with joy. 'I'm going to give you an education, mate,' he threatened her. 'I'm going to teach you how to talk.'

Jack, Vince, Jo-Ann, and the Raving Revvers

JOHN WAIN

••••

Looking through the window, Jack saw the bus from Macclesfield draw up and Jo-Ann get out. She was always on that bus, the one that arrived at ten past eleven. In the two weeks he had been working at the Jolly Farmer, Jack had got into the habit of watching for her arrival.

She came into the bar and went through to the back to hang her coat up. Jack was already in position behind the bar with his white jacket on.

'Hello, Jo-Ann,' Jack said as she went past him.

'Hello,' she said, her tone light and casual but quite friendly.

Jack always greeted her when she arrived and it was the only time he ever spoke to her first, without waiting to be spoken to. Jack looked up to Jo-Ann and never tried to get familiar with her. You had to be eighteen to work in a bar and Jack was just turned eighteen. It was his first bar job and he wanted to hang on to it if he could. Jo-Ann was twenty and besides that, she was very pretty: slender and elegant and very dark. She nearly always wore blue. She had a blue dress and an exactly matching blue head-band which came about half-way up her forehead. She was one of those girls who are so dark and so pale-skinned that any hair, anywhere on their bodies, is very conspicuous. Jo-Ann's arms had a very faint, very thin crop of jet-black hair on them. She could easily have waxed them away or something, but they were so scanty that she just didn't bother. She left them alone. Jack thought she was right about this. It made her long slender arms look even more beautiful. More natural. About anything that concerned the way she looked, Jo-Ann never made a mistake.

She came out of the staff cloakroom now, cool and fresh in spite of the heat. But Jack knew that before they finished their first spell of work, at two-thirty, Jo-Ann would be having to pause, whenever she could snatch a few seconds, to dab away little beads of sweat from just below her hairline and that dark patches would have appeared under her arms. Jack would be the same. He didn't go home, as Jo-Ann did, between closing at two-thirty and reopening at six, so he brought a clean shirt to work every day. It was two-shirt weather. The air-conditioning couldn't cope, even though Mr Petheridge kept saying it was a New and Improved Version.

As for Jo-Ann, she always appeared for the evening spell in a completely changed outfit, fresh from top to toe. She must have had a whole row of dresses in that enchanting shade of blue. She was a girl who really looked after herself.

'I s'pose we'll get the usual rush,' said Jo-Ann, staring out at the hot yellow sunlight.

'It's to be expected,' said Jack. 'If the weather cools down it'll drop back. They won't mind staying in town then.'

To understand this story you have to go back to the

fierce summer of 1983, when the whole of England fried and sweltered in a six-week heat-wave. Men, women, children and animals forgot what cool air felt like. Every few days there would be an isolated thunderstorm that drenched everything within its local range, but nine-tenths of the moisture was immediately drawn up into the air by the heat, and hung about in a sticky cloud until it was burnt away altogether.

The Jolly Farmer, a fine old building, stood on high ground near the border of North Staffordshire with Derbyshire. Even up here it was not cool, but the air was more tolerable than in the brick ovens that the local towns had become, places like Leek and Macclesfield. So people got into their cars every lunch-time and drove out here. Even if they only had an hour for lunch and the drive took them fifteen minutes each way, it was worth it to be able to relax in the garden of the Jolly Farmer with a cool drink and a few sandwiches or a ploughman's.

It was fine for them, and it was fine for Mr Petheridge, the licensee. But it was rough on Jo-Ann and Jack. The place got terribly crowded, with customers three or four deep round the bar. Their hands just couldn't move fast enough. People had to wait and they got bad-tempered.

To Mr Petheridge, of course, the ringing of the till was sweet music. He was an ambitious man who, in the three years he had been running the Jolly Farmer, had enlarged the place and put in all sorts of new equipment and generally brought it up to what he called Today's Standards. That was how Mr Petheridge talked—in short, emphasized phrases. If you had been writing down what he said, you would have had to put capital letters at the beginning of the key words.

As far as Jack could tell, Mr Petheridge approved of him. He particularly took note of how early Jack arrived at work. They did not officially open till eleven, and even then there was never much business before twelve or twelve-fifteen. Jack arrived very early, about nine. This was to beat the heat. He had to cycle eight miles to work from the town where he lived, and once the sun got up it was intolerable to try to pedal a bike up those long steep rises. So Jack got up early and biked out while it was still cool. He didn't mind the journey. He was used to cycling, and living round here taught you not to be afraid of a few hills. Going home at night, after the pub closed, was cool and dark and delicious. Swooping down the long hills with the night air streaming gently over his neck and chest, Jack felt that the exhausting heat of the day was worth it, for the contrast.

This particular day was as hot as ever. The heat-wave was into its third week and had, if anything, intensified. They seemed to have more work than ever. The two ladies who worked in the kitchen, doing the rolls and sandwiches and salads, were bad-tempered with the heat and overwork. Jo-Ann was grimly silent, slogging on. She switched on her mechanical smile when she served a customer, but as soon as no one was looking at her—when she turned and bent down, for instance, to get some more ice-cubes out of the refrigerator—she very decidedly switched it off again. In the first slack minute they had had since about twenty past twelve—and it was now two-fifteen—she perched on a stool, adjusted her blue headband with a limp gesture, and said, 'This place is getting to be a madhouse.'

'Yes,' Jack said.

'And the trouble is I don't belong in a madhouse. I'm not daft. Not yet anyway.'

'It's like the notice up in Mr Petheridge's office,' Jack said. Mr Petheridge had a notice above his desk that read, 'You Don't Have to be Mad to Work Here but it Helps.'

'Mr Petheridge,' she said, 'will have to do something else in his office apart from putting bloody silly notices up. He'll have to hand out more wages and take on some more bloody staff.'

It was the first time Jack had heard Jo-Ann use an improper word, let alone twice in two sentences. It showed she was getting very fed up.

When they closed at half past two, Mr Petheridge came into the bar. Jack was sitting on a bar stool, very slowly wiping his glasses, and Jo-Ann was draped over the cash register. Mr Petheridge stood there looking at them for a moment, considering. He was long and thin and had a well-tended moustache and highly polished shoes.

'Another busy session, eh?' he said.

'Busy isn't the word,' said Jo-Ann shortly.

'What is the word, then?' said Mr Petheridge.

'Murder, that's what it is, blue murder. There's just not enough pairs of hands. The length of time we've had to keep some of 'em waiting, the place is going to lose all its custom.'

Jo-Ann was too tired and frazzled to bother to be polite to Mr Petheridge. If he had sacked her on the spot she would hardly have noticed. But of course he had too much sense to do anything of the kind. He smiled as if something was giving him secret satisfaction.

'In That Case,' he said, 'you'll be Interested to Know,

Jo-Ann, that I am engaging Additional Bar Staff, to the Number of One.'

'Big deal,' Jo-Ann said. 'When does this number of one start?'

'Right Away,' said Mr Petheridge calmly. 'After the Formality of a Brief Interview this evening, he'll Report for Work in the morning.'

Jack wondered how Mr Petheridge was so sure he was going to take on this person, whoever he was, if he hadn't interviewed him yet. But he said nothing, just put down the glass he had been wiping very quietly and exactly in its right place. As if his question had been uttered aloud Mr Petheridge answered it.

'I didn't advertise the job,' he said. 'I made enquiries through Trade Channels. Rang up a Few People Who Knew. I told them we needed someone with Cocktail Experience.'

Jack felt disturbed at this. He knew it was his weak area. He had been learning the simpler parts of the job pretty fast, and by now he could pull a pint of beer as quickly as Jo-Ann could, but the cocktails often stumped him. He had to ask Jo-Ann to deal with them, which of course meant that he never did get any Cocktail Experience.

'Vincent,' said Mr Petheridge, 'that's his name. Vincent has Cocktail Experience. He's had a year over in Manchester. At the Empress.'

Jack had never heard of this place, whatever it might be, but presumably they sold cocktails there and this Vincent was some smooth operator who knew all their names and could shake them up and all that.

'Well, if he can stand up straight and hold a glass, and give the right change,' said Jo-Ann, 'he'll be better than nothing.'

'I think I can promise you,' said Mr Petheridge smoothly, 'that he'll be Very Much Better. All he has to do is to show up for a chat with me at six this evening, and not do anything to Put My Back Up, and tomorrow lunch-time we'll be One to the Good.'

'I suppose it's a temporary job he's getting?' Jo-Ann asked carelessly.

'The Staffing Arrangements,' said Mr Petheridge, allowing his gaze to rest on Jack for a moment, 'are Always Under Review.'

Jo-Ann took the bus in the afternoon to the place where she lived or sometimes to one of the local towns to go shopping, and caught another bus back at six o'clock. Jack, for his part, did not bother to go home. It was too far, and he was all right where he was. He had his meals in the kitchen and in the afternoon he was free to wander out into the quietly slumbering landscape.

On this particular afternoon, though, his spell of idling was not so pleasant as usual. His mind kept returning to the thought of this Vincent, and how much of a threat he would turn out to be. Mr Petheridge would hardly keep the two of them on when the end of the season came, and if this Vincent was a Clever Dick from the big city, he might have no trouble in easing Jack out.

Well, he told himself, the only thing he could do was work steadily, do his best at all times, and just let the chips fall where they may. Perhaps this Vincent was not so marvellous after all. A lot would depend on what Jo-Ann thought of him. Mr Petheridge was bound to take her opinion into account.

So he tried to take it calmly, but all the same he made it his business to be hanging about in the bar, pretending

102

to check the level of washing-up liquid and do little jobs of that kind, from about ten minutes to six. Then, as always happens, he found one or two things that actually did need to be done, and his attention became absorbed in them until, for a few minutes, he forgot to think about Vincent at all.

At about two minutes to six the noise began to make itself heard, first in the distance, then getting rapidly nearer. It was an urgent, high-pitched, rasping noise, as if someone was using a circular saw to cut through a sheet of metal, but doing it in a great hurry.

Jack looked out into the yard. He was just in time to see a motor cycle whirl in at frightening speed, heeling over at a racing angle, through the old gateway from which the gate had long since been removed. He could just make out, as the machine flashed by the window, that it was of the kind that are built up very high from the ground, as if designed to go at full speed over rough country, and that the exhaust pipe, doubtless for the same reason, seemed to run along the top of the engine rather than down below, and was covered with a perforated metal guard to stop it from burning the rider's leg. This rider wore a huge helmet and a zip-up nylon jacket in vivid scarlet. As Jack stared through the window, the motor cycle, still travelling fast but now slowing, came back into his field of vision. It had described a complete circle round the inn yard. The rider squeezed the brakes and brought it rocking to a standstill. The front suspension made a panting sound as the engine fell silent.

The rider swung off his machine and pulled it backwards on to its stand, where it stood gently fuming to itself in the sudden silence. Jack watched as the rider took off his helmet and started towards the main entrance. Was this Vincent? Or a customer? As the young man went past him, very close but oblivious of Jack's stare, Jack felt certain it must be Vincent. His rather heavy, fleshy face, under its thatch of dark hair, wore the purposeful expression of one who has come to get a job, not the relaxed expression that goes with stopping on the road for a drink.

Vincent, yes, certainly Vincent, disappeared from the window in the direction of the main entrance. Jack went back behind the bar, ready to serve the customers who had not yet come in. As he stood there, waiting to meet Vincent, Jo-Ann came in from the kitchen entrance.

'Well, I suppose that's him,' she said.

'Did you see him?' asked Jack.

'No, but I heard him. What an almighty racket. Still, I suppose it doesn't matter how he gets here as long as he's some use *when* he's here.'

Then Mr Petheridge came into the bar, leading Vincent. Full-face, Vincent looked even more assured than he did in profile. His eyes looked out at the world as if he had summed up any possible competition and dismissed it in advance.

'Vincent, These Two will be your Co-Workers,' said Mr Petheridge. He introduced them. 'This is Jo-Ann. And this is Jack.'

'Vince,' Vincent said.

'What?' said Mr Petheridge, slightly taken aback.

'Vince. I'm called Vince.'

'Your Previous Employers called you Vincent.'

'Yeah, well, Vincent's what I'm called on official forms and that. But it's Vince. My name.'

'Hello, Vince,' said Jo-Ann. Her smile was wary.

'When are you starting? You'll find plenty to do, I can tell you that.'

'I'll leave you to Get Acquainted,' said Mr Petheridge. 'Twelve o'clock tomorrow, then, Vincent. Vince.' He walked away rapidly.

Vince shot a look after him as if he were about to say something satirical, but instead he turned to Jo-Ann.

'What's the job like? Hang on, though—I might as well be a customer while I still can. From tomorrow I belong on your side of the bar, so let me have a drink while I can.'

'There's nothing to stop the bar help from buying themselves a drink now and then,' Jo-Ann said.

'Not the same,' said Vince with that calm assurance. He drew up a stool. 'I'll have a dry Martini,' he said. 'Ice and a twist of lemon. And what can I order for you?'

'Not this early,' Jo-Ann said. 'I can't start drinking this early, with an evening's work in front of me.'

'Go on, it won't hurt you.'

'I know what'll hurt me and what won't,' she said.

Vince gave her a we'll-see-about-that look. He paid for his drink, sipped it, and seemed disposed to go on making conversation with Jo-Ann. Jack wished some more customers would come in.

'How d'you get here?' Vince asked her.

'On the bus.'

Vince shook his head in disbelief. 'Where from?'

'Macclesfield.'

'All that way on the bus? Twice every day?'

'Four times,' she said. 'If you reckon twice each way.'

'*Four times*?' Vince allowed his glance to rest on Jack for a second. 'How about you, mate?'

'Jack,' Jack said.

'How about you, Jack? How d'you get here?'

'On a bike,' Jack said.

'A bike? I didn't see one. Where d'you keep it?'

'It's outside, in the yard. I just lean it against the wall.'

Vince shook his head. 'I didn't see one. What make is it?'

'Raleigh,' Jack said. 'I'd rather have an old bike of good make than—'

'Raleigh? What kind is that then? How many c.c.?'

'None,' Jack said. 'No c.c. It's a push-bike.'

'A push-bike?' Vince set down his glass. 'One of those things you get up on and pedal yourself along? With your feet? At about ten miles an hour?'

'One of them, yes.'

For the first time, Vince looked attentively at Jack.

'How far d'you come?'

'About eight miles.'

'Well,' Vince said. 'Now I've seen it all.' He turned back to Jo-Ann and said, 'I could give you a lift.'

'I'm not into motor bikes, I haven't got all the gear.'

'I'll lend you a helmet. And you won't need any other gear, not this weather. Where d'you live? Shall I come for you tomorrow?'

'No. I'm not riding on one of those things. They're dangerous.'

Vince drained his Martini glass and set it down on the bar with a decisive movement. 'If you want to live a safe life,' he said, 'the only way is to stay in bed all the time. And they tell me accidents will happen even there.'

The heat-wave sweltered on. If anything the temperature actually rose, and the ground became more parched and

106

cracked. Finally a day arrived when Jack could hardly bring himself to venture out of the Jolly Farmer to have his afternoon wander in the open country. He stood in the shade just inside the kitchen door and looked out at the hard dazzle of the inn yard, which ended in a straight line just in front of his feet, as if daring him to try to walk across it and survive.

He stepped out into the glare, screwing up his eyes, moving slowly because he did not want to start sweating. He got about five hundred yards from the Jolly Farmer before being forced to sink down in the shadow cast by a small hut at the angle where two fields met. As he sat there, letting his body cool off, he heard a voice that seemed to come from above his left ear.

He was right, that was where it did come from, and the speaker—he saw, craning round—was asking him, 'Did you see that bird?'

'What bird?' Jack asked.

'That goldfinch. He'd been feeding on the tops of thistles. I'd been watching him for, oh, seven, eight minutes. Then he suddenly flew away, right over your head. I'm pretty certain it was a male.'

'Oh,' Jack said. He felt an impulse to run away. The stranger had something of a mad look about him. Very tall and thin, wearing a lightweight zip-up jacket, stone-coloured trousers also lightweight, and a frayed straw hat to shade his eyes, he was not very much like anyone Jack had ever seen before; in some ways not like a human being at all; more like a bird, a tall wading bird. Jack had a book at home that someone had given him when he was a kid. It had pictures of animals and fish and birds in it. He suddenly remembered the egret. This man was like an egret, an ageing human egret. Even his pale-coloured clothes corresponded to an egret's white feathers.

Jack now saw that the man had a pair of binoculars slung round his neck. A bird-watcher, of course. That was where the gentle madness came from.

'You never quite know what you'll see up here,' the man went on. 'Have you ever seen a dipper?'

'Well, not that I know of,' Jack said. 'I mean, I might have seen one and not—'

'You wouldn't have any difficulty recognizing a dipper,' the man said. 'They're really extraordinary birds. A kind of moorland water-hen. They have very distinctive habits. They walk under water, for instance—can you beat that? They actually walk into the stream and let it close over their heads and just walk straight on. To see if there's anything worth eating on the bottom.'

It must be nice, Jack thought, this weather. He would like to be a dipper, just for one week. 'They must have to keep their eyes open in the water,' he said.

'Well, of course they do,' the man said. 'All birds that gather food under water have to do that. When a cormorant dives he has to keep his eyes open for quite long periods in *salt* water. We couldn't do that.'

He looked at Jack rather sternly, as if he had caught him trying to rob the birds of the credit due to their achievements, to undervalue the marvellous things they could do. As if Jack was somehow not being fair to the birds. This, Jack thought, was unfair to *him*. He knew, damn it, that birds could do things we couldn't. We couldn't even *fly*, or build nests in trees, or catch flies in mid-air, let alone keep our eyes open in salt water.

'I know birds can do things,' he said. 'They can find

108

their way to Africa and come back to the very same nest. They can do all sorts of things.'

But the man seemed to have forgotten shooting that suspicious glance at Jack. He was immersed in his thoughts about the birds he had come there hoping to see.

'Of course it's an in-between time just now,' he said. 'The tail-end of the breeding season.'

'Yes,' Jack said. It seemed he ought to say something, and that was the least he could get away with.

They talked for a while longer, then the egret man moved on. Jack remained leaning against the wall of the hut, his feet in the yellow smouldering sunlight.

At the end of the afternoon, Jack walked slowly back to the Jolly Farmer. By six o'clock he had the bar tidied and organized and was wearing his white jacket. Idly, enjoying the feeling of having no work to do for those last few minutes, he stepped out into the yard. The sun's rays were steeply slanting now, walls and trees were throwing longer shadows and Jack could imagine the leaves and grass just beginning to recover a little after the long day's grilling. He stood still, blinking, enjoying the peace. Then the angry mosquito sound of Vince's motor bike began to reach his ears. In these still surroundings you could hear it, he guessed, about a mile away. When it got to within a quarter of a mile or so, the noise changed from a mosquito-buzz to the scream of a metal-saw. Another moment, and Vince whirled in through the gateway, braking, changing down, finally halting with a last jerk that made the bike bob up and down on its front suspension. Vince got off. On this exceptionally hot evening he was not wearing his nylon zipper jacket. Beneath the towering helmet, the upper half of his body was clad only in a T-shirt printed with the words, RAVING REVVERS.

'Hello, Vince,' Jack said. 'What's the T-shirt?'

Vince nodded briefly, beginning to unfasten his helmet.

'It's my T-shirt. I'm wearing it.'

'Yes, but I mean, what's Raving Revvers?'

'Outfit I go riding with,' said Vince and moved on into the pub.

He was evidently not in a mood to talk to Jack, which was fairly typical of his attitude. He seemed to have no particular dislike of Jack. He never said anything offensive to him. He simply behaved, for the most part, as if Jack did not exist.

He was quite different with Jo-Ann, of course, and if Jack had had much curiosity to know about the Raving Revvers he would have had it well satisfied by the end of that evening.

Vince took his time about getting into his white shirt and barman's jacket; when Jo-Ann arrived at five past six, he was still standing around in his T-shirt.

'What's that then, Vince?' Jo-Ann asked, nodding towards his chest. 'A club or something?'

'Not what you'd call a club,' said Vince. 'We don't have membership cards and a rule book and subscriptions and all that lark. It's just a few of the lads that've got bikes and know how to handle them, like. We had these printed for a laugh. I'll get you one if you want.'

'What would I be doing with one? I'm not a Raving Revver.'

'You ought to come along with us. It's a good laugh.'

'Not my scene,' she said. 'Motor bikes and me don't mix.'

'What we do,' he went on, ignoring her dismissal of the topic, 'is we all meet somewhere when we got a bit of time off. We pick on a bit of rough country—steep slopes, heather growing so you can't see the rocks, bits of marsh where you don't expect 'em, dried-up beds of rivers full of stones, that kind of caper. And we do, like, orienteering. Pick on something we can see from a distance, like the top of a hill or something, a couple of miles off, and race to it. Everyone picks out his own route.'

'You must be always falling off,' she said with a look of mild distaste.

'Yeah, well, we take a few tumbles and that's how we learn not to be frightened of them. And it's good. Teaches you how to handle your bike.'

'I suppose it's useful,' she said disdainfully, 'if you want to be Eddie Kidd or somebody.'

Jack, watching unobtrusively from the other end of the bar, could see that Vince was needled by this last remark. Whatever mental picture of himself Vince carried around in his head, it would not be of an Eddie Kidd perched on a motor bike and taking a flying leap over half-a-dozen London buses. He would admire anyone with Eddie Kidd's nerve, but his own self-image would be of someone more sophisticated, someone who knew about cocktails and pitching a smooth line to girls.

What was more, Vince was undeniably narked at Jo-Ann's steady refusal to accept a lift with him on her way to work and back. She would have nothing to do with his skeletal, high-built, screaming bike. She said she didn't like the noise and she knew it would splash oil on to her clothes. Opening the refrigerator door and taking out a tray of ice-cubes, Jack listened for what Vince would say next.

'Eddie Kidd, nothing,' Vince said. 'There's more than one face to motor cycling. A bike like the one I've got outside, all right, fine, it's specialized, see? You get going up a rough track with the old Revvers on an ordinary bike and you'll be flat on your back in a ditch in five minutes. But I got my eye on a bike that's different altogether. Smooth. Purrs along. Big wide comfortable seats, no need to dress up in special gear, all sealed in, no oil splashing about. It's a Harley-Davidson Powerglide. Not new of course. They cost about five thousand new. But it's been looked after. Showroom condition. Every part replaced that showed any trace of wear. Had my eye on it a long time. I could get it with a down payment and two years to pay off. You wouldn't turn your nose up if I called round for you on *that*.'

'I don't know whether I would or not. I haven't seen it yet.'

'This bar,' said Mr Petheridge, suddenly coming through the door, 'is an ideal Venue for the customers to come and hold discussions about their cars and their motor cycles and What Have You. The customers, Vincent. Not the staff. The staff are Here to Work.'

'Right, Mr Petheridge,' Vincent said. He went out through the door at the back of the bar to get his white shirt and jacket. As he went past where Jack was standing he could be heard to say, quietly, 'Pig-faced old git.' Heard, that is, by Jack, not by Mr Petheridge.

As he cycled home that evening through the hot, glimmering landscape, pedalling very slowly along the level stretches, getting off and walking when the gradients were against him, and then sailing downhill with the wind caressing his face and head and cooling his chest, Jack had time to think over the situation at the Jolly Farmer. It looked to him pretty much like stalemate. Vincent had seemed the kind of thrusting, invading personality who would alter everything, taking no time at all to destroy the calm balance of their lives. But it did not seem to be happening. He did not appear to be getting very far with Jo-Ann. And Mr Petheridge showed no definite signs of preferring Vince to Jack. The dark hint of a threat about the staffing situation being Always Under Review, which meant in plain English that one or other of them would be sacked at the end of the summer, remained just that: a hint.

Then came the next push from Vince. And this time he really did succeed in altering the situation. It happened three or four days later. The morning opening time was about five minutes away, and Jack was in the wash-room, getting ready to go behind the bar, when he heard a sound from outside, a sound familiar and yet unfamiliar, a Vince-noise but not the usual one.

He went outside. There, in the sunlight, Vince stood behind a large and stately motor cycle. It was painted a glossy black except for the handlebars and wheel-rims, which were silver. The engine and the two exhaust pipes were not silver but more the colour of aluminium. Picked out in elegant gold lettering were the words HARLEY-DAVIDSON. The bike was leaning on a stand that jutted out from one side, as casually as a strong man lying on the ground and supporting himself on one elbow. It seemed to have an unusual length from front to rear, giving an impression of spaciousness, borne out by its broad tyres and wide comfortable saddles for driver and passenger. As Jack silently looked on from the doorway, Vince bent over the bike and made some minute adjustment. As he did so the bus drew up in the road outside and Jo-Ann got off. She came on into the yard.

'Well, well!' she said, halting.

'Like it?' Vince asked nonchalantly.

'Well,' Jo-Ann conceded, 'it's an improvement on that rattle-trap you had before.'

'Oh, I still got that,' Vince corrected her. 'I keep that for running round with the lads. Different bikes, different jobs. That's for rough stuff. This is for smooth stuff.'

'Must have set you back a bit,' she said.

'Put the first payment down last night. Like I was telling you. The bloke's giving me two years to pay off.'

'Two *years*? It'll have come to pieces by then.'

'Not this baby,' Vince said confidently. 'Here, get on—I'll show you how smooth she goes.'

'Get on? Are you mad? It's time to start work. Customers'll be—'

Vince looked over towards the pub and saw Jack standing in the doorway.

'Just a couple of minutes,' he said invitingly. 'I really mean, just a few yards down the road and straight back—five minutes at the outside. Jack'll fill in for us. Hey, Jack, serve anyone that comes in—we'll be right back.'

What does he expect me to do, Jack thought, with anyone who comes in, except serve them? Keep them waiting? Ask them to go for a ride on the back of my bike?

Vince swung the Harley-Davidson off its stand and held it steady on its two fat tyres. Jo-Ann climbed daintily on to the pillion seat. She seemed very much at home there, almost a mascot. Her dark hair gleamed in the sunlight, as glossy as coal.

Vince got astride. He pressed a self-starter and the engine began its throbbing. Vince glanced back at Jo-Ann to make sure she was ready. They purred off through the gateway and down the road.

Jack went slowly into the bar. It seemed very dark in there after the bright sunlight outside. He polished two glasses that didn't need polishing. Then he checked the level of the washing-up liquid. He knew it was all right but he checked it anyway. He felt too restless to sit and do nothing. No customers came in.

This new development had him worried. Vince was really after Jo-Ann. What was more, he was beginning to get results. If he could get her on to the bike, he could take her anywhere he wanted to take her. That was half the battle. What was more, Vince had undertaken to make regular payments on this super-bike for two years: which must mean that he was absolutely counting on being in work. When the season ended and the bar staff had to be reduced, Vince was gambling just about everything he had on being kept on. He was gambling, that meant, on Jack's being made redundant.

Yes, Vince was going to fight. But with what weapons? So long as Jack did his job all right and was friendly with the customers and got along with Mr Petheridge, how could Vince possibly get at him?

Jack didn't know. And that was precisely what made him feel uneasy.

The heat-wave was now in its fourth or fifth week. Jack hadn't been counting. All he knew was that it was beginning to tell on him. There were times when the heat seemed to press down on his skull and cook his brain to a useless mash. He would forget things that he knew perfectly well but couldn't, at that moment, retrieve.

At this rate, Vince would take over Jack's job for certain. Things got worse all the time. One thundery evening (if only a thunderstorm *would* break, but it never did) two young men drew up outside in a smart fast car and came in. They had two girls with them, the kind of girls who got themselves called 'dolly-birds'. Jack asked them what they wanted. The two blokes both had gin and tonic with lemon and ice, but the girls couldn't make up their minds, and after a discussion one of them said she would have a Black Russian. Jack had never heard of a Black Russian. He looked round for help, but Jo-Ann was busy at the other end of the bar. Only Vince was in earshot and Jack did not want to ask Vince.

'A Black Russian?' Jack said to the dolly-bird. 'Er, I'm not quite sure if we've got any . . . ' His voice trailed off. He had been hoping to prompt her into saying what the ingredients were. Then the other one stuck her oar in and said, 'And I'll have a Pina-colada.'

'Jo-Ann,' Jack called in a quiet but urgent voice, 'Jo-Ann, could you spare a minute?'

Jo-Ann was busy. The faint black down on her ivory arms caught the lamplight as she moved her hands rapidly back and forth, handing out glasses and change.

Vince moved over and said to the dolly-bird, 'A Pina-colada was it?'

'Yes,' she said.

'You're not going to believe this,' Vince said, 'but we haven't got a coconut in the place.'

'No coconut?' said one of the young men in mock incredulity.

'Don't get much call for 'em out here,' said Vince. He made a gesture of the head that indicated two things at once; first, that he considered the neighbourhood of the Jolly Farmer to be the ultimate tundra, and second that he was sure these four all shared that opinion. 'I can't do you a Pina-colada,' he said to the dolly-bird, 'but we can put on a nice Brandy Alexander. Or a Harvey Wallbanger.'

She chose a Harvey Wallbanger and the one who had chosen a Black Russian changed her mind and had one too, and Jack had to stand there and watch Vince put in the vodka, the galiana, the orange juice and expertly shake them up in the mixer.

'Delicious,' one of the dolly-birds said to Vince. Then she looked across at Jack and said, 'You know—I don't believe *he* knows how to mix cocktails.'

'Him?' said Vince lightly. 'He's not into cocktails. He's more the mild and bitter end of the business. Old-fashioned in his tastes.' In his 'You won't believe this' voice he added, 'Rides a push-bike.'

After this kind of encounter with Vince, Jack looked forward to his solitary sixteen miles a day in the saddle of his bike, and even more to his long afternoons of wandering and thinking. And on these afternoons he began to look forward to the chance of running across the tall man who looked like an egret wearing a straw hat. He liked to chat to this gentle, absorbed being, after the thrusting egotism of Vince and the cool, contained self-admiration of Jo-Ann.

As it happened, the next time they ran across each other

was on a Saturday afternoon. Jack was sitting with his back against a stone wall, listening to the chirping of a grasshopper somewhere nearby. He was hoping to locate the bright green body and long transverse jointed legs of the unwearingly trilling creature. But it was hard to tell what direction the sound came from: even, at times, to be sure that there was only one grasshopper and not several. He sat perfectly still. Presently he heard a deliberate, swishing footfall among the grass that might have been a cow moving to a fresh piece of pasture. It was in fact the slow, steady stride of the bird-watching man, walking beside the wall. He stopped when he saw Jack.

'If this were the kind of territory where one saw lizards,' he said, 'I'd be tempted to think of you as one. Certainly you're as predictable in your choice of habitat as a lizard. Always hugging the stones of a wall.'

'I like to be in the shade,' Jack said.

The man nodded. 'Quite right. Temperatures like these are excessive for the human body. The birds don't seem to mind, as long as they can get their moisture. Of course they can disperse heat through their feathers, wonderful things, feathers. They can keep you cool as well as warm. The most efficient skin covering ever known. I often think it's a pity human beings—'

'You must be getting near the end of your holiday,' Jack said to head him off.

'Too true,' the egret man said ruefully. 'This is the very last day. But,' the man went on, brightening, 'I feel very satisfied. The time's been well spent, very well spent indeed.' He took a small notebook from his pocket. 'I never thought I'd see half so many species. The variety in this one quite limited area has been ... unusual, I feel. It's exceeded my expectations.'

He opened the notebook and began to read off a list of the birds he had seen in his two weeks. Jack sat still, leaning his back against the wall, letting the birds' names wash through his head without trying to hold on to them. He had a very clear picture of the man striding along field paths, leaning over gates, sitting motionless among bushes, crouching among reeds and all the time watching and listening, watching and listening, for eight hours of every happy day.

'That's it,' said the man, closing the notebook with a triumphant snap. 'What d'you think of that, eh?'

'Smashing,' Jack said.

'It's certainly influenced my decision about the Annual Field Day,' the man said. 'I have the responsibility of organizing it this year, and at our last meeting before we finished for the summer they asked me to decide on the venue.'

'Oh?' said Jack vaguely. He supposed he would understand, sooner or later, what the man was talking about, and he also supposed that it didn't matter very much.

'The Amateur Ornithological Group,' the man said. 'We have an All-Comers' Field Day every year. Not in the nesting season, when some of our less experienced members might disturb breeding pairs, not after the migrants have all gone, but about half-way through September. Most people are back from holiday by then and they still want the odd day out of doors before the winter sets in.'

Jack tried to look interested.

'Of course it's a light-hearted occasion,' the man said. 'We turn everybody loose and at the end of the day we compare notes. We don't have any prizes, but we do announce the winning totals when we all get together for an evening meal.'

All of a sudden Jack stopped trying to look interested. An idea was beginning to take shape in his mind that made him look interested without any trouble at all.

'Evening meal?' he said. 'You have this day out and then you all go somewhere and eat together?'

'Yes, about half past six. A sort of high tea, really. We encourage people to bring their children—they're a nuisance in some ways but they're often quite good at bird-watching. Particularly when they can get competitive about it. And of course they like to eat fairly early. They build up an appetite, roaming about.'

Excitement gripped Jack. His throat felt tight.

'What day d'you have these outings? Saturday?'

'Sunday,' said the man. 'We find if we have it on a Saturday we get so few of the younger ones. The football season's started by then and—'

Jack was not listening. He was planning. Sunday was the ideal day: Mr Petheridge was always complaining about trade being slack on a Sunday night. He interrupted the man's monologue with another question.

'How many people would there be? More or less?'

'Hard to forecast exactly. But to give you a guide, the coach we usually hire, he's a local chap, seats forty-two and it's usually pretty full.'

Forty-two people. Say forty for a round figure.

'So you're holding it round here this year?' he said, his heart beating hard with anxiety.

'Most certainly we are. It's my decision and I think this is the best area I've investigated for years. Of the easily accessible ones, that is. It's got such a remarkable diversity of—'

120

'I can put you in the way of a good meal for them all, very reasonable,' Jack said. 'Solve your catering problems. At the Jolly Farmer, you know, just back there. I'll fix for you to talk to our governor. Mr Petheridge his name is. You can agree a price with him.'

'Well, I suppose there's no harm in—'

'Mr Petheridge wants the business. If you can guarantee him forty people sitting down to eat, he'll quote you a price and you won't get a lower one anywhere.'

'Well, it certainly sounds like a—'

'I'll fix it,' Jack said. 'You could come back with me now and see Mr Petheridge. Or you could give me your telephone number and I could ring you. I'll fix it.'

Mr Petheridge was pleased with Jack. He said he had shown initiative. Forty or so people booking in for a meal on a Sunday night at that time of year would Come In Very Handy.

He came into the bar to ask Jo-Ann if she would mind coming in at six o'clock on that Sunday evening rather than her usual time of seven o'clock. He said if she did it would enable the two kitchen ladies to get on with preparing the food while she waited at table. He knew she had not been taken on as a waitress and did not want to be one, but it was just for this one evening and he would Make it Worth Her While.

'If the restaurant side of the business really Takes Off,' he said, 'we can always get a full-time waitress. And who knows? With the right kind of marketing, it might Very Feasibly Take Off.'

When Mr Petheridge had gone Vince said, in a sullen voice, 'What's he rabbiting about? What's this marketing then?'

'Is it something you've been up to, Jack?' Jo-Ann asked. 'You been drumming up business?'

'I wouldn't say drumming up,' Jack said modestly. The feeling that both of them were looking at him, that after all these weeks he had their full attention, was a strange one and at that moment he could not have said whether he found it enjoyable or embarrassing. 'I just fixed for these forty people to eat here a week on Sunday night.'

'What forty people?' Vince demanded. 'You know forty people you can talk into coming here and eating?'

'No,' Jack said. 'I did it just through one person. He's the secretary of this . . . club they have.'

As he spoke he suddenly knew for certain that he must not, in front of Vince, use the word 'ornithology'. Vince would be sure to think it a piece of swank, an attempt to upstage him personally, to get back at him for knowing what a Harvey Wallbanger was.

So when Vince, still giving him his full attention, asked, 'Club? What club?' he just said, 'Bird-watchers.'

'Bird-watchers?' Vince gave a loud, sneering laugh. 'They ought to come with me and the lads on a Saturday night. We'd show them a thing or two about watching birds.'

Jack saw a slightly annoyed, impatient look cross Jo-Ann's face. 'Be your age, Vince,' she said shortly and bent to get some tonic water out of the refrigerator.

Jack also turned away, his face impassive but his heart joyful. Vince, by making that silly and obvious joke, had damaged his reputation as Joe Smooth from the big city. His mask of smart sophistication had slipped to one side. Perhaps, Jack thought, he was not such a formidable opponent after all.

Early on the Sunday morning when the coach arrived with the Ornithological Group, both Jack and Mr Petheridge were there to greet them. The egret man gathered everyone round him in the car park—parents, children, middle-aged couples, studenty young people, even some quite little kids—and gave them a briefing before they all set off. He had xeroxed a sketch map of the area showing the different kinds of habitat. They were to meet back at the pub at six, and he wished them, and himself, a good day. Then they set off, in every different direction, with their backpacks and binoculars. The egret man, with a last remark or two to Mr Petheridge and a friendly nod to Jack, strode off over the first ridge. Then they had all gone, and for the next eight hours it would be just an ordinary Sunday.

At a quarter to twelve Jack heard the purr of Vince's Powerglide, and looking out of the window he saw the contraption swoop in at the gate and vanish round the back of the building. Vince and Jo-Ann had arrived at work; that is, from Jack's point of view, they had taken on existence. When they rode away together, they entered a void into which Jack's imagination refused to follow them. He simply did not want to know how much time Jo-Ann spent with Vince, where they went or what they did.

Opening time arrived, customers began to come into the bar, and for a couple of hours Jack had not a moment to think of anything. It all passed off quite smoothly; nobody asked for one of those mysterious cocktails, it was all just beer and spirits and sherries and red and white wine by the glass, stuff he could handle in his sleep. 'Last orders, please,' Vince shouted.

Another stint nearly over. Then the long lazy afternoon and then the ornithologists' visit. Jack's hour of triumph.

First, though, there was lunch. Jack and Vince and Jo-Ann ate at two-fifteen on Sundays, after closing the bar, emptying the ashtrays and wiping down the tables. It was always a good meal and they took their time over it. But this afternoon they had barely sat down and started on the cold ham and chicken and scotch eggs and salad, with a light ale each on the house, when a familiar noise began to penetrate the building, it seemed from all sides.

It was a noise not quite as familiar as it had been a few weeks ago, but immediately recognizable for all that—the tearing, brain-severing screech of a 250 c.c. motor-cycle engine with the silencer taken off, the same sound as Vince's scrambler bike made, but multiplied two, three, half-a-dozen, fifteen times, as one rider after another arrived and went swooping around the empty car park or stood revving their engines in the pub yard.

'Friends of yours, Vince, sounds like,' said Jo-Ann calmly.

'It's the lads. They're out for a bit of a giggle. Stopped off on the way to see if I'm coming,' said Vince. He left the table.

Jo-Ann was eating unconcernedly. She even started chatting about something: Jack found he could not focus his mind enough to make out what. A feeling of anxiety, very close to dread, was slowly welling up inside him. The high-pitched snarling, repeated from one angry metallic throat after another, seemed to him threatening. It was like the sound of a pack of vengeful animals, circling the

124

building, waiting to tear him to pieces. Or, if not him, then his life. He could not have said why he felt this, but he did.

On the face of it there was no reason why the Raving Revvers should not stop by at Vince's place of work, just as he was due for a few hours off, to see whether he was coming along. That was all perfectly natural. But why was Vince so long with them? If all he had to do was tell them he wasn't coming, what was keeping him from his lunch?

Jack poured the light ale into his glass and drank a little. He looked down at his plate, but he could not eat. The menacing pack-howl from outside went on and on. Where was Vince?

All of a sudden the noise rose in pitch and volume to a concerted scream and then began to fade. The Revvers were moving off. On an impulse Jack pushed back his chair and hurried over to the window. Vince was standing by the gate. The last few riders were just going off and as each one passed Vince raised an arm and pointed, for all the world as if he were a commanding officer sending out troops on an assault mission. From where he stood Jack could not see the individual Revvers once they had dispersed.

Vince came back into the room and sat down at the table. Seeing Jack still standing by the window, he looked over inquisitively.

'Something interesting out there?'

'Well,' Jack said, 'it was quite a sight to see.'

'Nothing special,' Vince said, reaching for the sauce bottle. 'Just an ordinary little Sunday afternoon doodle.'

No one said anything else. They finished their meal,

Jack managing to swallow a little though he had no appetite, and took their dishes out to the kitchen.

Soon Jo-Ann and Vince rode off. Silence and heat took over the scene. Peace began to seep back into Jack's soul. Surely everything was all right? He wandered out into the yard. The afternoon was just like every other afternoon since he had started at the Jolly Farmer. All you could hear was the occasional swish of a car going past, and beyond that only the thin whine of a mosquito or something.

In the instant that Jack's ear took in the mosquito-whine, it grew louder and he realized that it was the note of one of the Revvers; probably a mile away but still perfectly audible. Presently it was joined by another, then by two or three more. The noise began to resemble Jack's notion of an aerial dogfight.

His heart pounding, he hurried up the ridge over which the egret man had set out. At the top was a wall. Jack climbed it. Now he could see across a wide expanse of moorland, heather and small patches of upland grazing. And wherever he looked he saw the bright-coloured helmet of a Revver, and caught the flash of metal as the Revver's bike swerved this way and that. Sometimes there would be two or three together, seeming to challenge one another to an impromptu race; more often it would be one rider, threading his purposeful way up a heather-covered slope or along a half-concealed sheep-track. As far as Jack's eyes could see in all directions, there the Revvers were, and there the tearing sound of their bikes came from. He now saw members of the ornithological party breaking cover, in ones or twos or small family groups, standing up and looking round them in attitudes that, even in the distance, indicated bewilderment. Occasionally a bird appeared in the sky, but always flying strongly and in a straight line, making for the horizon.

Jack did not know what to do. He stood close to the tree as if the nearness of its strong, solid shape could somehow help. But he knew that, as far as this immediate crisis went, nothing on earth could help him. The Ornithological Group's annual outing had been ruined and it was the Revvers, Vince's gang, who had ruined it. Jack could see of course that Vince must have set it up, but there was no way he could prove it. And even if he had been able to prove it, what would that show? Merely that Vince had outsmarted him. And by so doing Vince had made good his claim to be the one who was kept on in the job. The licensed trade needs people who have their wits about them. It does not need dreamers, people who get outwitted and left behind.

Jack stood by the tree for what seemed a long time. Ornithologists began to straggle past him down the slope towards the pub. One of the families that had come in their own car simply got into it and drove away, without waiting to speak to anyone, as if they were too fed up to want to discuss the matter.

One of the last to come down was the egret man, his face drawn into straight lines under that frayed straw hat. Jack guessed that he had tried to talk to the Revvers, to explain that it mattered a lot to him and his party to be left in peace for a few hours in this quite small area. If so, and Jack felt quite sure it must be so, it was obvious what kind of reception he had met with.

He disappeared into the pub, doubtless to telephone. Jack watched and waited. In about twenty minutes' time the coach in which the group had arrived that morning made a reappearance; they climbed in and went off to try to save something from the wreck of their September All-Comers' Field Day.

Jack moved up the ridge again, climbed over the wall and sat down with his back to it. All he wanted was to be invisible from the Jolly Farmer. He heard the swooping and crackling of the Revvers. They must have known that they had driven the ornithologists away. It was after six before they snorted away and their sound gradually died in the distance. Peace descended, peace that came too late and so brought with it a faint atmosphere of mockery.

When his watch showed five to seven, Jack forced himself down the slope and into the pub. Things were bad enough without failing to turn up to work. Jo-Ann was sitting in the bar.

'Oh, there you are,' she said. 'I've been here on my own since six o'clock. Turns out there was no need to get ready for that party after all. They never showed up.'

'Did you expect them to?' Jack asked.

'What d'you mean, expect them to? 'Course I did, it was a firm booking.'

Jo-Ann's face was very pretty but it told Jack nothing of what she might or might not be thinking. He would, he realized, never know whether she had been in Vince's confidence or not.

It was seven o'clock. Vince's Powerglide could be heard arriving. At that moment Mr Petheridge came into the bar.

'Well, that's it, Jo-Ann,' he said. 'I'll pay you for the extra time of course.'

'Thank you, Mr Petheridge,' she said. 'I'm sorry they didn't turn up.'

'So am I,' Mr Petheridge said. 'Of course it's understandable, with that racket going on. They came out here for a Bit of Peace and they found all Hell Let Loose.' He turned to Vince, who had appeared in the doorway. 'Those hot-rodders who've been roaring round here all afternoon,' he said. 'Are they people you know?'

Vince did not attempt to disown the Revvers. Cheerfully, he said, 'Oh, yes. The Raving Revvers. They're mates of mine. I go out with them sometimes.'

'But you didn't go this afternoon.'

'No,' Vince said. 'I was helping my brother to fix up his new video.'

'Did you know they were coming here today?' Mr Petheridge pursued.

Vince appeared to think for a moment. 'Well, yes, I knew,' he said. 'It's all been fixed for weeks and weeks. Only I didn't take much notice, like, because I knew I wasn't going to be with them this afternoon. I was helping my brother to fix his—'

'You knew,' said Mr Petheridge, speaking slowly, 'that this club or gang or whatever they are, would be riding round here all afternoon, making a noise like a flying circus, and you didn't Open Your Mouth?'

'Nobody asked me,' Vince said. 'I didn't think there was that much interest taken. I don't force my hobbies on people. I reckon, everyone to his own. I'd have said if anyone had asked me.'

Mr Petheridge turned his head and looked at Jack for a long time. Then he walked away and disappeared into his office.

Vince pulled down the zipper of his scarlet jacket. 'Well,' he said, 'let's get on with it.'

They got on with it.

Outside

R. M. LAMMING

●●●●

The yowl of a cat; a dustbin lid rattling in a yard; a car door slammed. The car's motor chirred, sputtered and died, chirred, sputtered and died.

Helen turned and looked at the clock. Its luminous green fingers moved in a series of sly jerks from luminous fleck to fleck across little spaces of darkness. Just gone half past one. Someone was out late. Some visitor, leaving. They had probably been at the Cohens' on the other side of the road. The Cohens liked to sit up into the small hours, clutching glasses of wine and talking, talking. She often saw them from her bedroom window, because they never drew their curtains. People in denim jeans, sprawled on convertible sofas among rubber plants and house palms.

The chirring and sputtering went on.

Four . . . five . . . He's going to make that battery flat!

Just then, the driver must have thought so, too. There was silence. Helen stared at the ceiling above the window. A wedge of light from a bedroom in the Cohens' house lit up the damp patch. Tonight, it looked like a miniature North America inhabited by ants, but she could turn it into several different things. She had a good imagination.

She could imagine that man in the car; he was staring at the ignition key; he sat stiffly, muttering curses. Then, for a moment, she changed him into a woman, and had her rummage in a handbag on the passenger seat for a packet of cigarettes.

The car began to chir again.

Helen thumped her pillows. 'Oh, get *on* with it!'

This time, the engine coughed, timidly at first, politely, then in earnest with a desperate raking of its throat—the sound of a struggle to dislodge something: a wickedly sharp stone. Next, it let out a roar, as though it meant to heave up everything: cylinder, pipes, nuts and bolts—and suddenly, it was breathing freely. It panted: she could sense a shudder passing through the whole engine. The driver wanted no more trouble. He revved up savagely, and the car wheezed out from the kerb. He did something brisk and bullying to the gears. A glare of headlights crossed her room as he drove away.

'Thank you, and good night!'

She tossed round beneath her duvet and stared at the wardrobe. Her room was icy—the central heating went off at eleven—cold air moved as she moved, touching her face, her neck. All the same, it was snug in bed. She stretched out her legs, then curled them up again.

I'm warm, that's the main thing. And I'm not upset.

She closed her eyes.

I might fall asleep, and I might not. It doesn't matter. Some very intelligent people never get a wink of sleep. Not every kind of brain needs it. That's what Dr Cowper said. But I will sleep. I will.

She lay motionless.

It didn't take long for the frown to come, forming with

131

relentless independence, line by line. A pain developed in the hard furrows above her nose. She opened her eyes.

That was silly. I wasn't relaxing.

Staring at the wardrobe. No help there. A solid, sensible piece of furniture, it woodenly insisted that nothing was worth a fuss, that there was a practical answer to everything. This wardrobe wasn't an ally: her lively, day-time clothes trapped inside it—they couldn't help her, either.

The worst of staying awake was the loneliness.

Her room darkened. That was the Cohens' light going out. Somewhere in a garden down the road, a dog was barking. Shut out, by the sounds of it. Out in the cold.

I'm better off than that!

She lay on her back, gazing at the window. It had become a thick slice of grey mist.

What was it like to be a dog? She tried to imagine the evenings spent head pressed down on a carpet, inches from the humans' feet, sponging up warmth from a gas fire, occasionally raising an eye to those green-blue flickers in the cupboard-on-sticks, which seemed to be the master of the humans; and hoping, all the time hoping, not to be remembered, not to be marched out round the block, then deposited for the night in the garden shed. 'There we go, boy! Settle down, now! Good night, boy!' Left amongst the cardboard boxes smelling of damp, the garden tools crusted with soil, paint tins, dust and paraffin cans. The human feet retreating into the house.

We've something in common! thought Helen. In her mind, this dog shut out for the night was small and grey with darker patches; it had come creeping out of the shed to stand by the kitchen door, shivering, its head hrown back as it barked at the upstairs windows. Helen often pictured sleep as a house, a grand one, with many doors and windows, all of them shut. Different doors and windows would open at different times to let people in, then shut again, and no one else had any trouble getting in, but Helen herself always chose the wrong door, the wrong window. Whichever she chose, invariably it would shut just before she reached it, and as she reached it, she could hear another door or window on the far side of the house snapping open, but when she reached it . . .

She tugged on the light cord, and grimaced at the sudden brightness. Ten to two. Although she could see it perfectly well where it was, she picked up the clock to look at it. People in movies did that: men and women who woke in the night stretched out a hand for their watch or bedside clock, picked it up and took a long time reading it—a series of actions which meant that either something important had happened, or was about to happen. Helen unconsciously copied these gestures of the cinema because they lent a tinge of drama to the monotony. They reminded her that life is full of events, and anyone who lives has to make their meaningful stories out of whatever comes. In the long deserts of her wakefulness, such reminders were invaluable.

Ten to two. If I can get to sleep before three, I'll have four whole hours . . . But I mustn't think about it. Dr Cowper said relax . . .

She set the clock down. It just fitted on to the bedside table in front of the Kleenex box and her battered transistor radio, which was wallet-size, a bright salmon pink, and very old, a present for her eighth birthday.

133

Some nights, she would let it crackle away from start to finish, from the moment she pulled up the duvet round her neck until she got out of bed in the morning: chatter chatter, jingle jingle, cheery professional voices notching off the minutes, all the quarter hours with deadly regularity. Jingle jingle, yes sir! That's the way the night goes! More often, like tonight, the thought of the transistor filled her with panic, as though switching it on were a guarantee that she wouldn't sleep.

What I could do with is an aspirin.

Keeping her eyes zipped up tight had brought on a headache. She lay dully. The aspirins were in the bathroom. It was no fun getting up in the cold, and anyway, she tried not to take too many aspirins. Besides, she hated shuffling along the landing, past her parents' door with the sound of her mother's snores ballooning back and forth across the room. It was worse still, passing her sister's door: dead silence. Rosie slept like a lump of rock, heavily and completely. But what she dreaded most was the house, hearing its sighs and creaks and rustles, noises that said: All the time it's reasonable for you to be awake, I do my job: I provide a home for you. But at this time of night, it's not reasonable; these are my own hours, when I'm myself, and what I am has nothing to do with you.

Oh yes, the house resented her intrusion.

Better stay put, she thought. *It's not such a bad headache. And I'm warm and comfortable.*

That dog had stopped barking. She felt a pang of envy.

I should think of myself as a cat. Creature of Isis, magical, mysterious, at home in the night. A night prowler.

Instead, she visualized the scrappy grey mongrel curled

up on his owners' bed, having won the argument. Allowed in, at last. As she watched him, his ears twitched. What did city dogs dream about? Not many rabbits and sheep around here. Cats, probably—but they might come in the nightmare category. Birds. Food and smells and love. What was it like, a dream made up entirely of smells?

Damn Lizzie Stubbs. Once a week at least, she would come up to Helen, usually in the morning break, and say, 'Hey, I had this really incredible dream last night . . . ' —and Lizzie was right about that. They *were* incredible. They sounded like made-up dreams in bad novels, although Helen never said so. She knew she was probably jealous.

Dreams.

Deep, glowing dreams with messages: Joseph's dream, all his brothers' sheaves of corn bowing down. The Pharaoh's dream: strange cattle rising out of a river, seven years of plenty, seven of famine. And Jacob's, the most beautiful dream of all: a ladder set between heaven and earth, angels ascending and descending.

Maybe she should switch off the light. Electric light in the very darkest hours seemed to lack essence: it was vampire light, that sucked strength out of her. She pulled on the cord, and the room blackened.

Only two more days to finish her history essay. Thinking of Lizzie Stubbs had nudged her memory.

This is ridiculous. If I can't sleep, I should be working, reading, doing something useful. But I am going to sleep . . .

She wriggled about until she found her favourite position; and being so warm, so pampered by the soft pillows, the duvet, it was not beyond the wildest realms

135

of possibility that at any moment she might stop being awake.

Behind her eyelids throbbed a batch of scarlet worms—the afterglow of the light: those worms came from the filament at the very heart of the bulb.

Dr Cowper's voice was saying gently: 'This insomnia of yours is becoming quite a problem, isn't it?'

No doubt about that.

Her mother's voice: 'Do you think she'll have it all her life, Doctor?'

'Let's hope not.'

Oh, let's hope not, let's hope not.

I'm falling asleep, thought Helen.

More yowling from the cat. Or maybe it was a different cat.

I'm just like everyone else, she thought. *At night, I sleep. Here I am, dozing off . . .*

One day, Mary Oxley had come up to her in the common room and asked, 'Is it true you've had only twelve hours' sleep in the last two weeks? That's what I've heard.'

'Yes. It's true.'

'How awful!' said Mary. 'I thought people went mad without sleep!'

Not every kind of brain needs it, said Dr Cowper.

She wondered what the time was.

But I won't look. I mustn't open my eyes.

'Asleep in one another's arms . . . ' The words came drifting down to her like twigs on a stream. Where from? Were they a quote from something? Or were they just another of those phrases like 'Happily ever after' that most people took for granted? Helen never took such words for granted. What would it be like to lie awake all

night, night after night, with someone sleeping soundly
beside her? Wouldn't she hate him? And how would *he*
feel? Could anyone ever put up with it, all her tossing
and turning and switching lights on and off? Maybe she
would never marry.

She looked at the clock.

Five past three. Oh, this was hopeless. Two and a half
more hours, then the wretched birds would start: tweet
tweet, good morning good morning.

Flinging back the duvet, she sat with her knees drawn
up. Freezing cold. Anyway, what was she doing? Restless,
just restless. She stood up, pulling the duvet over her
shoulders, and moved round objects, the bed, the chair,
making for the door.

Might as well get that aspirin . . .

But she changed her mind, and went to the window.

Standing up against the glass, she could tell how
different the cold outside the house was to the cold
inside. Inside, it was surly, sluggish yet chilling. Out
there—she rubbed a bright, black disc in the condensation on the window—out there, the cold had vitality,
it was creative.

Frost. A thin layer of whiteness lay on the road and
the privet hedges. The roofs of the houses opposite were
as grey as the windows; and looking down into the
garden, she saw that a greyish pretence of fibre-glass had
spread across the lawn, while in its centre, the iron
sundial had turned pewter-pale. Out beyond the roofs,
the darkness quivered with stars.

It was humbling. Nights—some of them, like this
one—were so beautiful, they shamed her out of unhappi-
ness. It was as though that house of sleep which she so
desperately longed to break into stood on a coast, on a

high cliff, and sometimes, while she was banging on windows or rattling doorknobs, she would glance round for no particular reason, and be astonished by a great ship passing on the sea: a silent, awesome vessel of lights and controlled power, following its course whether she cared to watch it or not.

Helen shivered. Looking at the stars convinced her just how cold she felt. She pulled the duvet about, trying to cover her ankles.

The Whites, who lived next door to the Cohens, had put out seven milk bottles, skittles of ice on the doorstep.

Somebody whistled.

A pure, penetrating sound, it was so in keeping with the frost that at first it didn't surprise her. For one long moment she listened, before she realized that whatever else frost might do—and she had read of ice, at least, creaking and groaning—it couldn't whistle.

Someone was out there.

Then she saw him: he had crossed from the bus stop at the corner, and was walking towards her: a man who wore a cap and a short jacket, dark trousers. It was no one she knew, somehow she was certain of that at once, and she found herself trying to explain him away—not with the gossipy interest of the day-time peeper round net curtains, but because it was natural in the middle of the night to want everything explained.

Maybe he needs a phone ... His car might have broken down ... He's looking for a light, someone still awake.

But he didn't have the air of a man whose car has broken down. He walked with his hands in his pockets, and as he came closer, Helen saw that in fact he was staring only at one house—at the Nicholsons' next door—and at one window: the room where Martin Nicholson slept, a rowdy kid, who at the last count owned thirty-nine computer games.

Maybe he's staying with the Nicholsons. I suppose they've given him Martin's room to sleep in.

She could feel for the kid: she knew what it was, to be pushed out of one's room for a stranger.

Then other ideas came crowding in.

He's forgotten the address. He's wondering if it's the right house. Either that, or he's worried in case he's kept the Nicholsons up . . .

She knew that feeling, too: dismayed anticipation by the front door, and what it was like to be greeted by a bleary-eyed stoic in a dressing gown with a mouth that was set in a hard crescent, tips to the earth: 'Had a nice time?'

'Yes, thank you; but I told you I'd be late. You shouldn't have waited up,' Helen would say. The response was always the same: 'You know we never go to sleep until you're home . . . '

The man was walking not fast, but with a kind of easy energy; and yet there was something odd about his movements; it was stealth, decided Helen, and she thought she understood the reason: one's own footsteps on an empty road can sound depressingly lonely.

Well, he wasn't as alone as he thought. She was glad he was out there, someone else wide awake; not that she wanted *him* to discover that *she* was there, at the window; as he came level with the house, she drew back, anxious to avoid for them both the unpleasant jolt of such a thing, waiting for him to pass. But he didn't pass, and in the end, she couldn't resist looking down again.

The man had stopped. He stood in the road, hands still

139

in his pockets, his gaze still fixed on Martin Nicholson's window; and from the way he stood, feet apart, cap tilted back, he had apparently come to more than a pause while he found his key. The truth was—an impression which had crept up slowly on Helen was now impossible to avoid—he seemed to be watching Martin Nicholson's window for a signal.

He whistled again.

'*Of course! He doesn't have a key, because he meant to come back hours ago . . . and Martin must be in there after all. Rather than ring the bell, he's trying to wake up the kid . . . He must be very cold*, thought Helen.

This time, he whistled softly. He held a single note for as long as it takes to count to five, then let it curve abruptly upwards. The silence which followed felt ice-sharp, and soon, Helen became aware of her own breath—clumsy, muffled little noises brushing against the window.

Only then did it occur to her that she was watching a thief.

Rubbish.

Her heart began a panicky thumping. It wasn't rubbish. On the contrary, it was as good an explanation as any. It would account for why he stood like that with his hands in his pockets, trying to look so casual when he was, in fact, very tense, cat-alert.

A man in his mid-twenties, the face he turned to the window was intelligent, and urgent.

Night prowler.

Casing the joint! The phrase came conveniently to mind, postponing things. *He won't do anything tonight. I can go back to bed. I'll tell someone in the morning.*

Another of those long, quiet whistles—

And a horrible certainty fell on Helen: someone had broken into the Nicholsons' house already. This man was a look-out. Naturally, thieves plan things. They have systems. They divide their labours. And if this man's partner had broken in already, the crime wasn't going to be tomorrow night, or next week. It was now.

I can't just stand here . . .

She didn't move. Slowly, the circle she had cleared on the misted glass was beginning to blur.

Outside, the man in the road suddenly lowered his eyes, and took a couple of steps towards the Nicholsons' gate, but once on the pavement, he stopped again; and now he was staring not at an upstairs window, but across the garden . . .

His partner must be coming out . . . Would a thief come out by the front door? Well, why not? Who's going to stop him at three o'clock in the morning? . . . I should do something.

The trouble was, Helen realized, she didn't believe in any of it. The stranger by the gate certainly looked suspicious, but he didn't have the look of a villain. Probably, very few thieves did. In his tense expression, there was suppressed hopefulness, she would almost have said a suppressed happiness, that went very oddly with the thought of crime. The trouble was, she realized, like the man, she was waiting for something to happen. Something that would prove her theories wrong.

But the moment I'm sure I'm not wrong . . . I'll phone the police . . . And I'd better wake up Dad.

That would be embarrassing. No amount of banging on the door would do it; he could sleep through anything—the way her mother snored, he had to. And as for her mother, when *she* slept, all her being was

141

concentrated on those snores, as if she'd bring disaster on the family if she missed one out by mistake: a knock on the door would never wake *her*. Helen would have no choice but to march in, right up to the bed, and yell. She hated that. She had done it once when Rosie was sick, and again, when her uncle had phoned at six-fifteen in the morning to say that her aunt had just been taken to hospital; and both times, despite the excitement of the emergency which forced her to wake them, Helen had been shocked by the sight of her parents. Lying there in the sheets, they had resembled nothing so much as huge, dishevelled babies, helpless and—to be honest—ugly. Then, when her dad had woken up, he had put a hand across his mouth because he had taken his dentures out, and he had blinked up at her apologetically, shyly. It was horrible.

Still, there was no way round it: she was beginning to resign herself—when footsteps sounded on a garden path, running.

The partner.

She hadn't heard a door open—but of course not: expert thieves are skilled in the arts of silence. On the other hand—

On the other hand, why was an expert thief making such a din, running on concrete in hard-soled shoes?

Forgetting caution, she pressed her forehead to the glass, and peering down across the hedge into the neighbours' garden, half-way to the gate she saw a girl.

Definitely not Mrs Nicholson, plump and inelegant with a permed head of black curls, who usually dressed in nondescript trousers and a duffel coat. This girl was slim, with hair that fell on her shoulders. She wore a beret and a three-quarters length coat tied at the waist.

The hem of her pencil skirt was just above her knees, and her shoes were high-heeled, chunky. It was a trend for the few, this look of the 1940s, a sophisticated one, which could have nothing to do with the homely Nicholsons.

A girl thief.

Helen's tidy notions slipped.

Out on the job, in clothes like that?

The girl was carrying a small, battered suitcase.

The loot? Surely between them they could carry more!

Now the man had leapt forward. He opened the wrought iron gate; its ornate catch clicked sharply, and the girl ran out into his arms. Still clutching the case, she flung her free arm round his neck. They kissed.

Lovers. Lovers in the night with a suitcase.

I've got it all wrong. The Nicholsons' must be the house on the other side . . .

Helen knew it wasn't. What she was seeing was simply inexplicable.

It was also highly romantic. To have called these lovers happy would have been an understatement. Just by the way they held each other, she could tell that being apart had been an evil for them, a time filled with dark menace; and now they stood together, quietly waiting for strength, while waves of relief broke over them. She could tell that the house was already forgotten: whatever—or whoever—in there had been the cause of all this, this running away in the night, the threat couldn't touch them now. They were invulnerable. They looked it. Invulnerable—and defenceless, she decided. Odd, that they should be both, as if they could never be hurt again, but they could be swept off the face of the earth with no great effort: a puff of wind might do it. As she watched them, Helen felt she understood why Hollywood lovers never looked quite right. With their thought-out scripts and clever directors, they knew too much. They knew where to put their feet, and how not to bump their faces—and what would be asked of them next. Reality was different; it was bewildered. In all the movements of the man and the girl on the pavement, their arms around each other, the sleeves of their coats straining, there was a lack of preparedness, and that was why they looked so easy to blow away. Yet somehow it was also why they looked defiant, issuing a challenge to the universe: together we can face anything life chucks at us, no matter how bad it is. But so long as we're together, surely life can only be good.

They're a bit old-fashioned, thought Helen. He was holding the girl very protectively. *It must be amazing, to be loved like that.*

The half-wish nudged her back into a sudden, awkward awareness of herself.

Not my style, spying on lovers . . .

It wasn't, but she made no attempt to move. No use pretending otherwise; as long as they stood there, she knew she was going to watch. She felt caught up in something more than curiosity. It was a tangle of pain, drawing her towards tears.

She was glad when the man and the girl began to talk. The man took charge of the suitcase. Holding hands, they turned down the road.

Then, finally, when they had their backs to her, Helen moved—but only to rub the condensation off the window. In the next second, she wished she hadn't. They stopped. They glanced round, and not at the Nicholsons'.

Me. They're looking at me. She felt sick. *They knew*

144

I was watching. They must think me a pathetic little sneak . . .

But the lovers smiled at her without a trace of mockery. She saw that their faces were radiant, and very pale. Ice-pale.

They waved. Helen waved back. For a moment, she felt warm.

They left no footprints in the frost, and before they reached the corner, they had gone from the road—but when it came to that, none of it surprised her. She could have noticed earlier. There were several tell-tale signs; something about their breath, for instance.

She breathed out, and watched a vapour cloud the glass. Outside, where it was certainly even colder, there had been nothing.

I've fallen asleep by the window. I've been dreaming of ghosts. I'm asleep. I finally made it.

She swayed towards the glass, and, to test her theory, willed the Cohens' house to vanish. It stayed where it was.

'Try not to keep a watch on yourself,' said Dr Cowper's voice, gently warning.

This is mad. I really am standing by the window . . .

But all the rest had to be dream. When the lovers had waved, she had known exactly what they meant, not in the way she usually imagined things, but because their words had come, silently spoken, dream-real:

Please, they had said, share our happiness.

And because they asked, of course one did. A little.

Ghosts in a dream, inviting her: Come in part of the way, at least.

Sleep did the same thing sometimes, opening a door when she least expected it.

145

Bed. Before the cold wakes me up completely . . .

Obviously, she was almost awake. Her feet were chilled. The bed, when she got there, gave a deadly welcome, like a snow-drift.

A dream . . . an incredible dream for Lizzie Stubbs . . .

Only, it wasn't the sort that Lizzie would appreciate.

'I saw a girl come out of the house next door with a suitcase. There was this man on the pavement. They kissed. Then they walked down the road. They waved to me. Then they disappeared.'

'Well?' Lizzie would say. 'That doesn't sound like much.'

'I know it doesn't.'

No, decided Helen; she lay cocooned in her duvet; *it's not a dream for Lizzie.*

And with that sorted out, she did at last fall asleep.

Chimborazo, Cotopaxi ...

FRANCES THOMAS

●●●●

The sky was bright as knives, but there was no sun. The huge bowl of the amphitheatre was flooded with harsh shadowless light. Row upon row, tier upon tier, a tyrant's monument. The white sand had been newly combed, but there was no one there. No one. He was alone.

He was alone until the shadow fell, dark at his shoulder ...

'Get up, Moffat, get up, you silly sod! It's ten past!'

'Shut up, Levine ... Christsake, leave me alone will you? Ouch. *Ouch.*'

'That's better. Up you get.'

'Is it really ten past?'

'Would I lie to you? I say, Simon, these socks don't half stink. Can't your mum afford an extra pair?'

'Piss off, Levine.'

'Where's your sense of humour this morning, eh?'

'Look, shut up, will you? It's just that I'm not ... Listen, Levine?'

'I'm listening. Only get a move on.'

'It's just ... Oh hell, I don't know. I keep ... I keep ... '

'Spit it out.'

'I keep getting dreams. The same ones over and over again. But you can't feel things in dreams, can you?'

Levine threw back his head and guffawed. 'So that's why you didn't want to get up this morning!'

'No, you nurd, I didn't mean that.'

'Oh great! Poor old Moffat! Poor innocent little Moffat! And another nasty surprise for Matron when she comes to change the sheets!'

'Look, shut up will you, I didn't mean that.'

'I had one of those the other week. Coo-or! It was that new lab assistant in her white coat. "Let's do an experiment," she says. Boy, was that a dream!'

'No, I keep telling you, I didn't mean . . . Oh, what the hell. Let's go.'

He had never seen the amphitheatre before. But the dream was always the same, no matter where it took place. Once it was in an empty street, high walls sprouting weeds. Once on the rainswept steps of a huge cathedral, once a deserted railway station, with a soot-streaked roof. None of them were real places. None of them felt like real places.

Only the shadow was real, falling at his shoulder, and the man who cast it. A pleasant enough face it was, smiling. Bony, angular, fair hair flopping boyishly forward. 'I want to help you, Simon. Nice to meet you, Simon.' Then the face moved forward, still smiling, so that the beaky nose and the big teeth filled his vision. Soon only the smile was there, like the Cheshire cat, a smile without a face. And that's when it began to hurt. 'I want to help you . . . ' But he couldn't breathe. And the more he struggled, the worse it was. A slow spreading

148

blackness that would overwhelm him, as he gasped and gasped for the breath that wouldn't come . . .

But you couldn't. Not in a dream. You couldn't feel all that in a dream, could you?

'Come along, you lads. Get moving. Your parents don't pay hundreds of pounds a year to have you lounging around like unemployment statistics.'

'What do they pay hundreds of pounds for, then, sir?' said Palmer cheekily.

'Lord knows,' said Mr Kerridge. 'The alchemist's quest, I suppose.'

'Sir?' said Palmer.

'Base metal into gold, stupid,' said Levine.

'Exactly, young Levine. A transmutation which in the case of most of you will never be achieved I fear. *Moffat!*'

'Sir?'

'Are you with us, Moffat? Or are you off in some grubby little world of your own?'

'Sorry, sir.'

'He's been getting these dreams,' sniggered Levine.

'Shut up, Levine.'

'Has he indeed? What dreams, Moffat? Wild dreams of erotic fantasy? A thousand virgins all taking their knickers down?'

The class giggled. Mr Kerridge began to get into his stride.

'Lissom young lovelies panting at your feet? Glorious girls falling down before you?'

Mr Kerridge had published a novel ten years ago and it hadn't done very well. The rumours were that his second had been rejected. Simon sighed and roused himself. You had to beat Mr Kerridge at his own game.

149

'I don't have to dream about that, sir, thank you.'

The class giggled again. Conway licked a thumb and stuck an imaginary point on to an imaginary wall. Mr Kerridge scowled slightly. There was a scandal going round the school at the moment about his pretty wife and the geography master.

'Glad to hear it, Moffat. Of course girls today have rather poor eyesight, don't they?'

But Kerridge had definitely lost that round. The class giggled weakly.

'Talking about dreams,' went on Mr Kerridge, 'brings us to the subject of today's poems. The nature of poetic imagination. Before we go on to poor old Samuel Taylor and his junkies' paradise . . . ' He paused slightly for the laughter which didn't happen. Not to be deprived of his effect, he raised an eyebrow in the direction of Jenkins. Jenkins always looked slightly bemused which made him a good stooge for Kerridge's witticisms. 'Oh yes, he was, Jenkins. Samuel Taylor was a raging junkie. Of course they called it laudanum in his day and *said* it was medicinal. But you and I know better, don't we? Kubla Khan was written in . . . ' Kerridge searched for the correct modern phrase, ' . . . in an opium trip, Jenkins.'

'But sir,' said Levine, who had read a book about it, 'he was in a lot of pain, wasn't he? It really *was* medicinal for him, wasn't it?'

Simon sighed and propped his chin in his hands. The nasty taste left by the dream would not go. Holidays were only two weeks away, and he thought of Levine's sister, Charlotte. All the Levines were clever, and Charlotte was supposed to be the cleverest. Some sort of musical genius. But she was pretty, too, and she fancied Simon. Everyone said so, even Levine. Simon fancied her too, but something daunted him. Perhaps it was Charlotte's intelligence. She would know too much. He wanted to hide his thoughts these days. Only the man in the dream knew, the man who smiled and tried to kill him.

You couldn't, in a dream, feel real pain, could you?

'Well, of course,' Kerridge was disconcerted by Levine. 'Of course, that was his story and he was sticking to it. But it's a strange and complex thing, imagination. Without it, where would we be? Where would we be, Moffat?'

'I don't know, sir.'

'I didn't think you did. Come on, sit up. Stop doing your famous impression of the Lady of the Camellias, and think. Imagination, Moffat. Probably the real point of departure between Man and the animals. People say animals can't feel, of course, but they're wrong there. Anyone who's seen a dog pining for its master or a cat looking for its kittens can testify to that. Animals *can* feel. But the difference is, they can't imagine. The dog can't imagine what loneliness *might* be like. The human being can. And does. It adds a whole dimension. Without imagination, our lives would be bleak and meaningless.'

Kerridge paused. Simon wanted to ask him, what if the things you imagined all seemed to be unpleasant, then what? Where did that leave you in relation to the animals? But how could you talk like that to Kerridge with his sarcasm? He would turn the whole thing into a joke at Simon's expense.

'Look, for example,' Kerridge went on, 'at this one on page 19. You probably read it in the first year. But it's an extraordinary, and I think, very sensitive account of what imagination can do at a crucial age, adolescence, a time when, to many people, fantasy can be more real than what is actually happening.'

He began to read, in his resonant, English-teacher voice:

> 'When I was but thirteen or so,
> I went into a golden land,
> Chimborazo, Cotopaxi
> Took me by the hand.'

'More bacon, dear?'

Home. That meant warm pyjamas, crisp bacon and eggs that didn't taste like rubber. It meant his own room where his airfix models and adventure stories surrounded him like comfortable aunts and uncles. It meant being 'dear' and not 'Moffat'. It meant someone to make his bed and being able to lock the lavatory door.

'No thanks.'

'Oh look, there's a lovely piece here. It'll only go to waste.'

'No thanks. Oh, all right.'

'Simon?'

'Yeah?'

'Did your father manage to have a word last night?'

'A word? What about?'

His mother swallowed. 'Your report came yesterday. Simon, we're worried.'

'Oh, that.'

'Yes, that. The last thing I want to do, dear, is to nag you, but . . . '

> My father died, my brother too,
> They passed like fleeting dreams.

I stood where Popocatapetl
In the sunlight gleams . . .

'So naturally it's the first thing you *are* going to do.'

'Simon!'

'Sorry, Ma.'

'Well, you must admit, it isn't very good, is it?'

'No.'

'And it's not as if you were stupid, is it? I mean, if you were stupid, then we wouldn't mind, you know that.'

Oh yes, you would, dear parents. You'd mind. You'd mind like mad. I realized that right from kindergarten. I only got three for spelling, today, Mummy. Mummy, Nicholas did better than me in sums. Ah, you had to be an only child, an only child of slightly elderly parents to understand how to hurt. How to drive the knife in. No, thank you, Daddy. I don't want a microscope for Christmas. Can't I have an Action Man instead? But you didn't go doing that sort of thing too often. Usually, you took the microscope and the book on wildlife and pretended to enjoy them. You listened eagerly in the Science Museum and the Tower of London. And you made sure that next time, you beat Nicholas in sums and that you won the prize for the best project. And then you thought they might stop. But they didn't. Because once you'd set yourself up as a clever boy, then you had to live up to it. 'Daddy and I would like you to sit this entrance exam, darling. Now we shan't mind at all if you don't pass, but it's one of the best schools in England. Mr Miles says it's every bit as good as Eton or Harrow. We shan't worry at all. We only want you to do your best . . . '

We *only* want you to do your best! Had they ever

analysed that sentence? Did they realize what they asked? Well, he'd done his best. He'd passed, too. But still it didn't stop. 'Don't you worry about the fees, darling. After all, it's not as though we want fur coats and holidays abroad, is it? We'll manage. All we want is your happiness, Simon.'

So, if it's true, why do you do it? Why put me under interrogation every time I don't come up to scratch? Yes, it had been a bad report. But didn't they realize, any of them, that he couldn't keep it up for ever? He wasn't going to be a brain surgeon, or a physicist, or a Nobel prizewinner. He knew what happened to the second-rate when they worked their guts out. They ended up frustrated and bitter like old Kerridge.

What was the point? What was the point?

> *I walked in a great golden dream*
> *To and fro from school—*
> *Shining Popocatapetl*
> *The dusty streets did rule ...*

Last night, he had thought quite hard about his parents being dead. He thought about it quite often. Then his fantasies had started getting to grips with Charlotte Levine.

Chimborazo, Cotopaxi ... What would they find if they opened up his head like an egg and peered inside?

'So what now?' said Levine. With the next breath, he said casually, 'Our bill, please.' The waiter bowed. Waiters always bowed to Levine.

'Dancing,' said Nicola, Levine's girl. 'Let's go bopping.'

154

'Christ, no,' said Levine. 'Too much energy required.'

'It's a smashing night,' said Simon. 'We could go to the river.'

'I know,' said Levine. '"Alien." It's on again in Leicester Square.'

'Too far,' said Charlotte Levine.

'Nonsense,' said Levine. 'Five minutes in my nice new vroom-vroom.'

'Ooh yes,' squeaked Nicola. 'In Space No one Can Hear You Scream. Lovely. Ooh let's.'

'How kitsch,' said Charlotte. She looked across the table at Simon.

Simon did a quick calculation. He'd been humping boxes for a week in the local Safeway. He'd probably got just enough to pay his share of the bill and the bus home. But the cinema, especially a West End job, was beyond him. Levine got an allowance from his father.

'Not that rubbish, Char,' he said. 'Come for a walk.'

'I don't know,' said Charlotte. 'It might be fun, in a silly sort of way.'

'I'm offering you the river by moonlight, and you want to go to the pictures.'

Nicola giggled.

'What's everyone else want to do?' said Charlotte.

The bill came. Levine waved it discreetly towards Simon. Yes, it was all right. The result of one week's work would just pay for what he and Charlotte had consumed. No wonder the working classes hated the rich.

'Don't do what everyone else wants,' said Simon. 'Be original.'

'I want to see the film,' said Nicola.

'Oh, I don't know,' said Charlotte. 'It's too stuffy to sit in a movie.'

'Right,' said Simon. 'That's settled.'

Down by the river the sky was dramatically dark blue, and the lights that reflected off the water were as bright as a child's beads. Charlotte leaned on the stone parapet, sniffing the air. 'God, it's beautiful,' she said.

Simon felt that he was supposed to follow this by a compliment to her. She *was* very beautiful. But somehow he didn't want to say it.

'Tell me one thing, Simon,' she said, the unspoken compliment thickening the space between them, 'what exactly is it you want from life?'

Simon flinched. 'Why on earth is it that standing by rivers always makes people talk about Life-with-a-Capital-L?'

'Don't be cynical. It doesn't really suit you.'

'Oh, I don't know. I think it suits me rather well.'

'Martin always says that you could be really clever if only you bothered.'

'Amazing, isn't it, how other people always know more about you than you do yourself.'

'People don't always understand themselves so well, Simon.'

'Spare me this Freudian bullshit, right?'

'I think I can see things about you that you can't,' she pursued relentlessly.

'Such as what?' A dangerous opening, that, but vanity could not resist.

'Well. You come across all brittle and cynical but underneath I think you're very young and vulnerable.'

'Beneath His Cold Exterior . . . ' said Simon.

156

'There you are. You try to deflect me by turning it into a joke.'

'Women,' said Simon. 'They always want to save you. Why can't you accept that I'm just nasty?'

'Because I can't, that's why.'

'I'm a monster,' he said. 'Any moment now I'm going to take you in my arms and ravish you.'

She smiled, but moved imperceptibly away.

'Aren't you going to let me kiss you?' he said.

'How male chauvinist of you,' she said, coyly, 'to assume that it's a question of me *letting* you.'

'Well, prove that it isn't,' he said. He reached out and took her hand. 'You're very pretty,' he said. It wasn't so hard to say, the compliment, but he wished that he had not said it.

She stretched out his fingers and pretended to examine them. 'I suppose you have masses of girl-friends,' she said.

'Thousands. But I can always squeeze another one in if I try.'

'I'm quite house-trained,' she said.

'How busy are you these holidays?'

'That depends on you.'

'In that case,' he said, kissing her, 'then you are. Very busy.'

'Come round next week,' she said. 'The parents are away. I'll cook for you. I'm a good cook.'

'I'd like that.' Suddenly he was conscious of feeling happy.

That night, he had the dream again.

Outside his study the noise of boys was deafening. He switched up the transistor to try and drown the sound.

Conway stuck his head round the door. 'Sod off, Conway,' said Simon. Conway was a creep anyway.

'For God's sake,' said Conway, 'I was only going to pass on a message. I shan't bother now.'

'Then go and communicate with your navel instead. If you can stand the smell.'

'It was Levine,' said Conway with aggrieved dignity. 'He's looking for you. He's mad. I don't blame him.'

Conway closed the door behind him.

A letter from Charlotte lay on the desk. 'Please, Simon, please. Just see me and tell me *why*. It's being dropped without a word that's so horrible. So O.K., I know that's what men did in the old days when they had Had Their Way with you, but this isn't then. Is it? *Is it?* Simon, please tell me. So maybe I did make a fool of myself the other night on the phone but it won't happen again, I promise . . . '

Last summer belonged to another age.

She was well shot of him.

Levine came in without knocking and shut the door quietly. 'Right,' he said. 'I want a word.'

'Have two,' said Simon. 'Have three.'

'I'm serious, Moffat.'

Simon pushed Charlotte's letter out of sight. Levine wasn't looking at the letter anyway.

'If it's about Char, then I'm sorry about what happened, O.K.?'

'Sorry!' said Levine. '*Sorry!*'

'What more do you want? Blood?'

'Char hasn't stopped crying for a week. It's like Niagara Falls at home.'

'She'll get over it.'

158

'You reckon?'

'People always get over things.'

'Do they really?' said Levine.

'Besides it's none of your business.'

'*My* sister?'

'For God's sake, what's got into you? You sound like someone in a Victorian melodrama. *I say old chap, you've insulted my sister—*'

'Ha ha!'

Simon found that now he had started he could not stop. 'Of course that's what's really bugging you, isn't it? The fact that I've screwed your sister. That's what it is. You're jealous!'

'Oh, for God's sake! . . . '

Levine hit him in the mouth. But he was no sportsman and Simon had been junior boxing champion. Simon punched Levine in the stomach. He could feel the blood oozing through his teeth. Levine gasped and then rising to his feet, tried to hit Simon again and missed. Simon tried again and didn't miss. There was a crash as something rolled over. Levine's clenched face was very close to his. Simon hit him again.

The dream came now almost every night. A deserted city square, high grey walls, dark windows. A smell of dust. Could you smell dust in a dream? A dried-up fountain. Dead leaves rushing against stone. Then the man appearing very quietly behind him. Simon closed his eyes and waited.

A golden land.

'All right now,' said Mr Jeavons. 'Let's have your explanation and it had better be good.' Mr Jeavons was

Simon's housemaster. He was young, witty, and usually sympathetic.

'I'm sorry, sir.'

'Very good. You're sorry. Levine's got a broken nose and a face like a piece of raw liver and you're sorry.'

'I didn't mean to hurt him.'

'Dear God, then, Simon, what's it going to be like when you *do* mean to hurt someone?'

Simon opened his mouth to apologize once more, but closed it before he did.

'Come along then. Explanation time. Levine won't talk so it's down to you. What was it all about?'

Simon was silent.

'Your fault or his?'

'Mine, sir.'

'Very good. At last we begin to get somewhere. You know, it's funny. Last term you and Levine are as thick as thieves, and today, the first day of term, you start off by punching each other to oblivion. Why, Simon, why?'

'Sir, it was . . . '

'Yes?'

'Levine's sister, sir.'

'Charlotte? The violinist?'

'Yes. This holiday. We went out together.'

'And did Levine object to that?'

'No.'

'Well, what?'

'Well, she got . . . rather keen. And I . . . '

'Go on.'

'I . . . '

'You what?'

'I . . . ' Simon tried again.

'Did you sleep with her?'

160

'Yes.'

'Is that why Levine got mad?'

'Not just that, sir. I told her I didn't want to see her again.'

'You said she got "rather keen". Do you mean she was in love with you?'

Simon swallowed. 'I suppose so.'

'And you made her unhappy?'

Simon shrugged.

'Is she still unhappy?'

'I don't know. I guess so. Yes.'

'And that's why Levine's mad at you?'

'Yes.'

'Let me get this straight. You play around with Charlotte Levine, just for fun, get her into bed and then you ditch her. I've met Charlotte Levine,' said Mr Jeavons. 'She's worth ten of you, Simon.'

'Yes, sir.'

'If I was your age and she fell for me, I'd be over the moon.'

'Yes, sir.'

'But you go and treat her like some cheap little slag.'

'I didn't mean to hurt her. It wasn't like that.'

'Well, what was it like, Moffat? I'm waiting to hear.'

I didn't want her to fall in love with me. It was too much, another number like my parents getting hurt. I can't handle it. On my own, I'm stronger somehow . . .

And yet, why was it that he could say all this inside his head, but when he tried to put it into words all that came out was . . .

'I didn't want to get involved, sir.'

'I see. You didn't want to get involved. Simple, isn't

161

it. The cry of cowards throughout the centuries. Well, let me tell you, young man, if you want to play silly games, choose someone of your own emotional age to do it with. Leave adults like Charlotte Levine alone. Meanwhile, you've got some growing up to do. I should get on with it.'

'I want to help you,' the blond man said, smiling. 'You must let me help you, Simon.' He went on smiling as he lifted the knife.

The term went badly. His marks went down and down. Levine's nose healed with a bump in it which would be with him for life. They didn't talk to each other any more and Charlotte Levine stopped writing him letters. He didn't get too friendly with anyone else, and the other boys seemed to be giving him a wide berth. Well, let them. He imagined his parents dead. He couldn't think of any other way to get them off his back. He imagined himself making love to a dozen Charlotte Levines in a dozen different ways. He imagined hitting more people just as he had hit Levine. Had he enjoyed hitting Levine? He didn't know any more. He thought about setting fire to the school. He saw the slow, curling deaths of all the staff. Mr Jeavons was to suffer most of all.

It was getting on for the end of the school year. An English lesson and Mr Kerridge in fine sarcastic form. 'James Joyce. The first exponent of the modern idea that if you don't understand it, it must be good. All right? All right, Moffat? Having an interesting sulk there at the back?'

162

> *I dimly heard the master's voice*
> *And boys far-off at play.*
> *Chimborazo, Cotopaxi*
> *Had stolen me away . . .*

'No, sir.'

'Moffat, the Hamlet of the Lower Sixth. The Melancholy Pain.'

Someone giggled.

'Ha ha, very funny, sir,' said Simon.

Kerridge raised an eyebrow. He would not stop now.

'Well, Moffat. Do you have anything interesting to contribute on the general theme of *Finnegan's Wake*? You have of course read *Finnegan's Wake*, have you not?'

'No, sir.'

'Oh pardon me, Moffat. Do pardon me. I thought that the interesting display of silence to which you have been treating us over the last few weeks meant that we no longer had anything to teach you, that you knew it all. Isn't that so, Moffat?'

Simon felt the anger beginning to rise inside him.

'I haven't read *Finnegan's Wake*, sir.'

'No, you haven't have you? In fact you haven't done anything much recently, have you? Except thinking your own nasty little thoughts?'

I dimly heard . . .

'For Christ's sake, you wanker, just stop picking on me, will you?'

He stood up with a clatter. Everyone looked up in interest. He had nearly pushed his desk over, so he thought he might as well finish the job. It crashed against an empty desk in front. Pencils and folders scattered to the floor. As he went out, he swept the contents of Mr Kerridge's table to the floor too.

He heard someone snigger. Then he slammed the door so hard that the glass rattled.

This time it was the Headmaster. The Headmaster did not invite him to sit down.

'Quite frankly,' he said, 'we've had just about as much of you as we can take, lately. Fights, laziness, insolence. I won't stand for it, Moffat.'

Simon studied the edge of the Headmaster's desk. There was a photograph of his two laughing children and a tray with neatly sharpened pencils. One of them said 'Royal Wedding 1981'.

'I've spoken to your parents on the phone,' he went on. 'And they agree with me. They say you've been sullen, uncooperative and rude. A changed boy, is what your mother said.'

'Yes, sir.'

'Now, I happen to know that your parents have worked damned hard to send you here. They've made sacrifices. If I were to expel you, it would break their hearts.'

Simon looked up. He felt that he had half expected this.

The Headmaster seemed pleased to have some reaction. 'Does that surprise you, Moffat? Because that's the step we'd normally take when someone seems to be so set against the school as you are.'

He picked up a ballpoint pen and twiddled it in his fingers.

'But you see, Moffat, when I look at you, I see an unhappy boy, not a bad one. And I don't want to penalize anyone just for being unhappy. I'm going to make you an offer, Simon . . .'

Simon sat stiffly in the dusty plush waiting room. Heavy furniture carved from funereal mahogany stared down at him. But what else could he have done? 'It would break their hearts . . .' You couldn't resist that one, could you? The anger and the bitterness which had been part of him for so long were suddenly giving rise to panic. No, no, it's not the right thing to do . . . don't do this to me.

'Mr Moffat?' said the plump middle-aged receptionist blandly. How many of them did she see every year, twisting their hands in the blue armchair? 'This way, please, Mr Moffat.'

The room was empty. He waited in a high-backed chair of imitation leather. On the doctor's desk was a telephone, a clean blotter, and yet another photograph of laughing children. Was that supposed to be some indication of humanity, like Hitler kissing babies? The walls of the room were a neutral yellow beige, with a print of a Degas ballerina and an olive green carpet. As characterless as a hotel. But it was supposed to be, wasn't it? He wanted to run, to get out of there as quickly as he could. Blast his parents; blast their broken hearts. They would just have to put them together again without him . . .

But just as he was rising to go, the door began to open slowly, and he sat down, gripping the shiny, imitation leather chair. He could hear someone coming into the room, hear the slow measured tread, but he did not look up.

'Hello, Simon.'

And finally, he raised his eyes, as the blond man lowered himself into the chair at the other side of the wide desk, smiling . . .

ABOUT THE AUTHORS
• • • •

Jon Blake was born in 1954, near Reading. He went to school in Southampton, but only when forced to. After a spell as a drama student and a year selling carpets, he took a degree at York. Since then he has mainly been a teacher, although in his spare time he has played lead and bass in a variety of groups, and written six novels, four plays, and about thirty short stories. These can all be found on a shelf in his flat. His most famous work to date has been *World Times*, a modest newspaper he produced at the age of nine, which was featured on television.

Jane Gardam was born in North Yorkshire and spent much of her childhood on her grandparents' farm in West Cumberland before reading English at London University. After post-graduate research she worked as assistant literary editor on *Time and Tide*. She began publishing her work in 1970, writing at first mostly about children. Some of her early books (*A Long Way from Verona*, *Bilgewater*, *A Few Fair Days*) are published now on adult as well as children's lists. She was short-listed for the Booker Prize with *God on the Rocks* and won the Whitbread Award with *The*

Hollow Land. She has published several volumes of short stories and three stories, from *The Sidmouth Letters* and *The Pangs of Love*, have been made into films. *The Hollow Land* has been filmed for *Jackanory*.

R. M. Lamming was born in the Isle of Man in 1949. She was educated at a boarding school in North Wales and at St Anne's College, Oxford. Over the years she has contributed to various short story anthologies, and her first novel, *The Notebook of Gismondo Cavalletti*, published by Jonathan Cape in 1983, was awarded the David Higham Prize for Fiction.

Penelope Lively was born in Egypt and did not come to Britain until she was thirteen. She took a degree in History and then, she says, 'came late to writing— accidentally and on the way as I had thought to quite other things'. Her children's books include *The Ghost of Thomas Kempe* and *The Voyage of QV66*. She has published five novels, of which *Treasures of Time* won the Arts Council National Book Award for Fiction, and two collections of short stories. She has also written television plays, and a book about landscape called *The Presence of the Past* which she describes as 'a respectful tribute to the history of the English land- scape which I have found such a powerful inspiration.' In 1987 she won the Booker Prize for her novel, *Moon Tiger*.

Emma Smith was only twenty-four when her first book, *Maidens' Trip*, was published in 1948. The story of three young girls working a pair of canal boats between London Docks and Birmingham, it was based on her own wartime experiences; *Maidens' Trip* won the John Llewelyn Rhys Memorial Prize and her next novel, *The Far Cry*, also won a prize, the James Tait Black.

Several years later, after she had married and then been widowed, she began to write novels for children, among them *Emily's Voyage* and *No Way of Telling*.

Frances Thomas was born in Wales and now lives in North London. Her first novel, *The Blindfold Track*, was published by Macmillan in 1980 and won a Welsh Arts Council award. Since then she has written two teenage novels, *Dear Comrade* and *Zak*.

John Wain was born in 1925 in Stoke-on-Trent, Staffordshire, and educated locally and then at Oxford, where he has spent most of his life since. Poet, short-story writer, literary critic, dramatist, biographer, autobiographer and novelist, it was as the last of these that he first came to notice in the 1950s. His publications include *Poems 1949-1979*, a novel for young people, *Lizzie's Floating Shop*, and a novel for all people, *Young Shoulders*, which won the Whitbread Award for Fiction in 1982. He was awarded the C.B.E. in 1984.

Peggy Woodford was born in Assam, India, in 1937, and spent her first nine years there. She was educated in Guernsey and at Oxford. After working for BBC TV, she taught at a sixth-form college before turning to full-time writing. She has written several teenage novels including *The Girl with a Voice* and its sequel, *Love Me, Love Rome. Misfits* is the third anthology of short stories she has commissioned and edited.

Further Titles in Methuen Teens

While every effort is made to keep prices low, it is sometimes necessary to increase prices at short notice. Magnet Books reserve the right to show new retail prices on covers which may differ from those previously advertised in the text or elsewhere.

The prices shown below were correct at the time of going to press.

☐ 416 06252 0	Nick's October	Alison Prince £1.95
☐ 416 06232 6	Haunted	Judith St George £1.95
☐ 416 08082 0	The Teenagers' Handbook	
		Peter Murphy & Kitty Grime £1.95
☐ 416 08822 8	The Changeover	Margaret Mahy £1.95
☐ 416 06242 3	I'm Not Your Other Half	Caroline B. Cooney £1.95
☐ 416 06262 8	Badger	Anthony Masters £1.95
☐ 416 07292 5	Masque For A Queen	Moira Miller £1.95
☐ 416 08572 5	Rainbows Of The Gutter	Rukshana Smith £1.95
☐ 416 07432 4	Flight In Yiktor	André Norton £2.50
☐ 416 07422 7	Taking Terri Mueller	Norma Fox Mazer £1.95
☐ 416 03202 8	The Burning Land	Barbara & Scott Siegel £1.95
☐ 416 03192 7	Survivors	Barbara & Scott Siegel £1.95
☐ 416 09672 7	Misfits	Peggy Woodford £1.95
☐ 416 12022 9	Picture Me Falling In Love	June Foley £1.95
☐ 416 04022 5	Fire And Hemlock	Diana Wynne Jones £1.95

All these books are available at your bookshop or newsagent, or can be ordered direct from the publisher. Just tick the titles you want and fill in the form below.

Methuen Books Cash Sales Department
P.O. Box 11, Falmouth,
Cornwall TR10 9EN

Please send cheque or postal order, no currency, for purchaser price quoted and allow the following for postage and packing:

UK	60p for the first book, 25p for the second book and 15p for each additional book ordered to a maximum charge of £1.90.
BFPO and Eire	60p for the first book, 25p for the second book and 15p for each next seven books, thereafter 9p per book.
Overseas Customers	£1.25 for the first book, 75p for the second book and 28p for each subsequent title ordered.

NAME (Block letters) ....

ADDRESS ....

....